RIGHT FACE

THAT A SOCIETY NEEDS TO POPULATE

AF582523

VB KANDU

Copyright © VB KANDU
All Rights Reserved.

This book has been self-published with all reasonable efforts taken to make the material error-free by the author. No part of this book shall be used, reproduced in any manner whatsoever without written permission from the author, except in the case of brief quotations embodied in critical articles and reviews.

The Author of this book is solely responsible and liable for its content including but not limited to the views, representations, descriptions, statements, information, opinions and references ["Content"]. The Content of this book shall not constitute or be construed or deemed to reflect the opinion or expression of the Publisher or Editor. Neither the Publisher nor Editor endorse or approve the Content of this book or guarantee the reliability, accuracy or completeness of the Content published herein and do not make any representations or warranties of any kind, express or implied, including but not limited to the implied warranties of merchantability, fitness for a particular purpose. The Publisher and Editor shall not be liable whatsoever for any errors, omissions, whether such errors or omissions result from negligence, accident, or any other cause or claims for loss or damages of any kind, including without limitation, indirect or consequential loss or damage arising out of use, inability to use, or about the reliability, accuracy or sufficiency of the information contained in this book.

Made with ♥ on the Notion Press Platform
www.notionpress.com

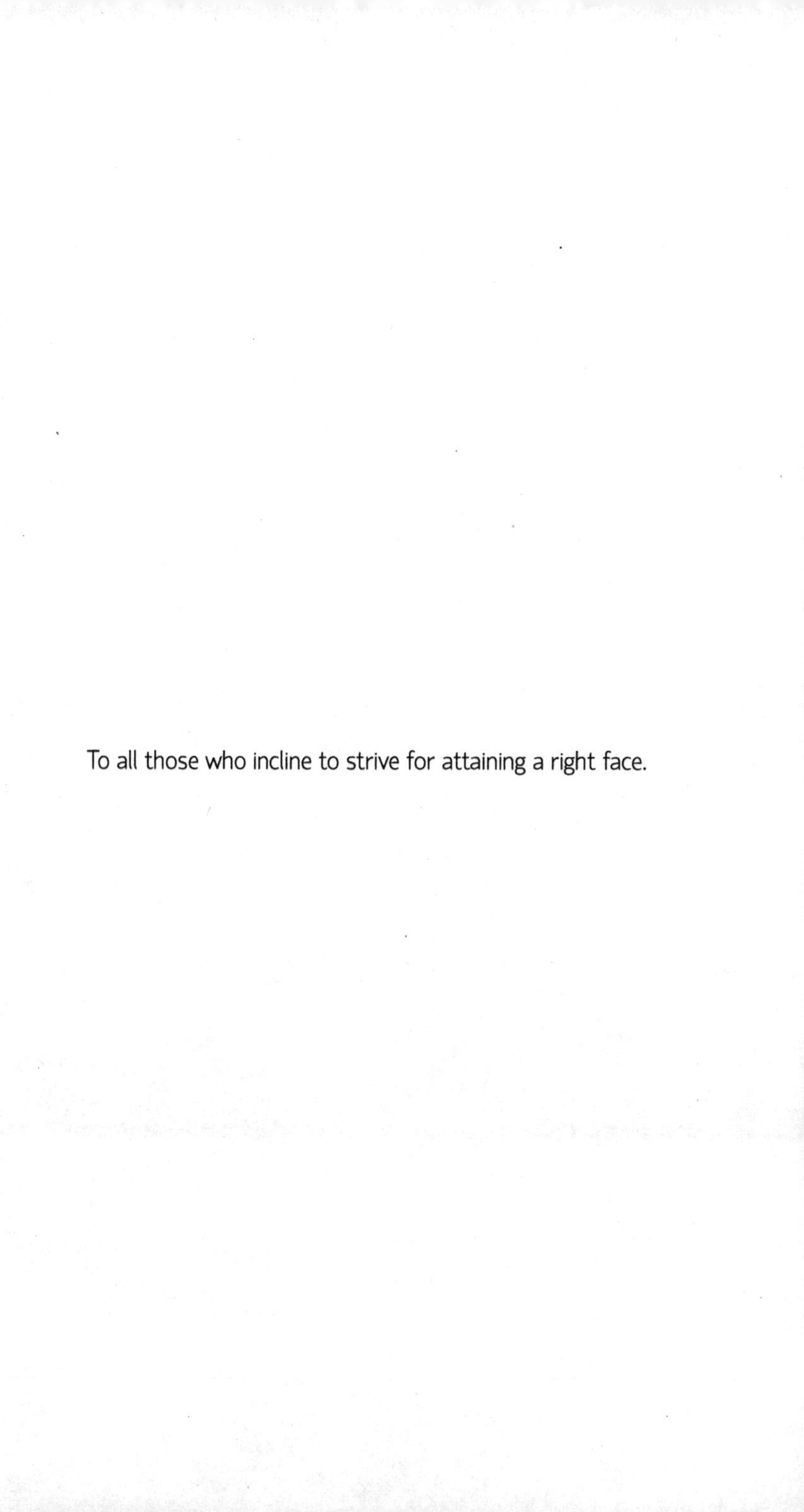

To all those who incline to strive for attaining a right face.

Contents

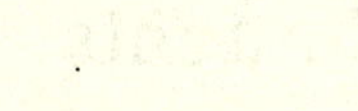

Acknowledgements

Thank all those who made it possible

CHAPTER ONE

December 31

11.55 PM.

The weather is chilly with a clear sky.

City Railway Station is abuzz with the usual jostling passenger traffic, arriving and departing trains amid the recorded voice of the announcer that is blaring through the speakers about the arrival and departure of the trains with the cut and paste information in the typical as-a-rule accent achieved in three languages at a stretch that enables the passengers well-attuned. Almost all the platforms are full of crowd as it is the peak time of the junction station for trains' movement to all directions.

Rahul got down from the local shuttle train on the sixth platform and started climbing up the foot-over bridge.

An express train has rushed on to the first platform and stopped with a jolt. Suddenly, there was a commotion on the first platform.

He heard people yelling that somebody was run over. He kept on climbing up the steps and looked towards the side where the sounds came from. He saw crowd gathering at a spot in the first platform. 'Something must have happened!', He thought.

He climbed down onto the first platform and without looking that side, moved towards the exit.

"Lucky fellow! Didn't see the new year!", somebody is saying loudly behind him with a baffling laugh to his own joke.

Rahul stepped out of the station and looked around without stopping. Actually, he wanted to travel by Metro service. Since the railway station was nearer than the nearest Metro station, he got into the local train which was about to start when he entered the boarding station.

The night is chilly but alive with high decibels of noise being generated by the rushing crowds near the City Railway Station. People are moving in all directions. The traffic seemed more than normal at this time. Vehicles are trying to pour through the human hurdles with blowing horns. The area is over-illuminated with the glittering, flooding and flashing lights of commercial sign boards in addition to the lighting coming from the shops, restaurants, small tea kiosks, box type cigarette and pan shops. He came out from the premises of the Railway Station.

Suddenly, everybody is yelling, "Happy New Year!", in chorus and hugging one another.

It seems, year by year, the trend of celebrating the New Year and particularly, the farewell night of the previous year is changing with introduction and following of new ways and methods of celebrations. The youth, who are engaged themselves in celebrations in all the corners of the City, seem planning in advance as to how much loud ruckus they could make on the eve of New Year.

Rahul stepped into the nearby Omega Hotel for a cup of *Irani* tea. Omega is a very old and popular restaurant nearer to the railway station which is famous for its Irani tea, cakes, snacks and biryanis. Since it is so adjacent to the Station and City Bus stop as well, it is always crowded. Now also, the hotel is jam packed with heavy rush as it is full of customers who gathered to have a sip of Irani tea or tasting the food or snacks on the occasion of bidding farewell to the old year and welcoming the New Year. After waiting for a ten minutes in the queue, he has got his cup. He liked its taste and hence, got one more. After finishing the second tea, he came out and lit a cigarette.

There is no difference in the atmosphere between inside and outside of the hotel. People are yelling with joy, sending messages and sharing wishes or cake pieces. Already bike riding drunken youth are creating flutter by rushing madly and shouting loudly.

He finished the cigarette and started to walk towards his rented house located in the nearby lane of about one and a half kilomitres.

A young Black in a blue jeans, who is standing at a few steps away and observing him keenly, also moved and followed him with a few meters distance.

Rahul reached to the end of the street where the three storeyed old building standing like a destined shelter for those who struggle to lead lives with less than enough income to meet their needs. One cannot identify what is the exterior color of the walls of the building as it was painted more than a decade ago but one can say it must be somewhere between pale brown and yellow with white patches here and there. The Black who followed him upto the building, stopped a few metres away in a dark corner and kept watching him.

Rahul opened the compound wall gate of the building and walked towards staircase as the building is not provided with lift facility. There is no basement for the building to park vehicles. The flats started from the ground floor itself. The open space inside the compound wall is full of bikes and bicycles parked wherever space is available. After a couple of minutes, he reached his room that appears from the outside like an old cat sitting prettily at a corner on the terrace of the building.

He opened the door and switched on the light and fan.

It is a small asbestos sheet roofed room with one small attached bathroom. The cot, though placed at the corner wall with the only small window, occupies half of the room space.

A small kitchen platform erected on the opposite side is being used to keep all his belongings like his suitcase, bags, a small water can etc. The shirts, pants and underwear he wore in the last one week are hanging on the hanger hooks fixed on the wall. The broom kept at a corner behind the door is almost worn out and ready to be thrown away as scrap. The floor is dusty as it would be swept only once in a week whenever it strikes to his mind. The iron cot is old which was left by the previous tenants. The mattress and the pillows seem lost their puffiness. The bed sheets and the pillow covers need an urgent wash.

Rahul is tired. His mind is simmering with oscillating thoughts over what happened since last afternoon. As there is nothing to do outside and there is no one accompanying him or nothing special is there to celebrate the New Year's Eve, he returned to his room. He stood in the middle of his room and looked around. The room is dirty and needs to be cleaned. But, he has lost interest and patience in attending routine things.

He switched off the light and threw himself onto the cot. He fell into deep sleep within a few seconds.

The young Black who was watching him from a dark corner of the by lane, waited for a minute and turned back after seeing the light went off in Rahul's room.

****

"Happy New Year Chintu! Sorry, I won't come now....better... you go to bed now..... It's too late..... I'll come in the morning.....okay.... good night!", Vinay Kumar, Inspector of Police, cut the call in his mobile after talking to his son and hurriedly attended the already ringing landline phone on his table.

On hearing the voice of Bhargav, the Assistant Commissioner of Police over the phone, his body too came into attention along with his voice.

"Vinay! You be on the patrolling in your area.... we got the information....drug parties are on the move all over the city.... search anybody on any iota of suspicion...right?" , ACP ordered.

"Yes Sir, already one team is on patrol Sir...I will move right now Sir...I will immediately inform the control room Sir...Yes Sir....No Sir...We have three informers Sir....Okay Sir...Sir...Happy new year Sir.... thank you Sir....Okay Sir!", Vinay Kumar cradled the receiver with the satisfaction of wishing the boss and getting good reciprocation too.

Vinay is in his early forties who has grown up in the ladder of his career with the result oriented tasks assigned by the superiors. He joined in the police department as a Sub-Inspector. Now, he is empaneled for elevation as Deputy Superintendent of Police. He has been waiting for that to happen for the last one and a half years. But, the Administrative delays are making him to wait for more and more time than he expected.

It is already 12.30 AM.

A small celebration of cake cutting has already started in his station. For the last two years, with the increasing night duties on important occasions, he has been missing to celebrate New Year with his family particularly, with his children.

He came out of his station with his team and got into the vehicle.

"Sir, better making rounds in and around Jamboree Hills area...we can easily catch hold at least one or two young asses with the stuff there!" Sub-Inspector Raghu told him as if telling the top secret.

He is the most reliable aide for Vinay in all the operations he takes up.

"See...Raghu....with the increasing money out of these increasing software jobs, some guys, particularly some idiots are getting addicted to all the vices that come along with money....and...causing head ache for us.....this city is really turning worse with growing population, money and pubs", Vinay sighed, getting himself adjusted in the front seat of the vehicle.

City has already become a hub for drugs supply and consumption. The consumption has become rampant among the youth and the City is said to have become the headquarters for the drug mafia.

The City Police Commissioner is worrying over the increasing rate of drug related cases. As drug traffickers are able to sneak into the city with the stuff, police are struggling to tackle the cases as well as the attack from media and opposition parties.

However, Police have been trying to vie down the drug mafia with new ways and means including increasing use of technology and human effort in the form of trained informers. Nowadays, ACP -Bhargav, who has been assigned the task of dealing with drug cases has become more popular as an expert in dealing cases related to drugs and narcotics. Inspector Vinay is one of the officers in the team he got ready for working meticulously in search operations and solving the drug related cases.

As the New Year is a great occasion for drug sales and consumption, he has already made arrangements for grounding search squads in all corners of the City. Inspector Vinay Kumar is one of his reliable aides involved in the search operations and dealing with drug related cases.

"Hello Salman!, Happy New Year!, we have already moved", Vinay Kumar wished over his mobile one of his helpers who tip off as and when they smell drug trafficking or peddling in their assigned areas. The vehicle is already moving towards such an area.

"Happy New Year Sir!", Salman responded.

"Sir, already I got an eye on certain persons...we are following them...we suspect that since this morning sales were at higher side...I am sure they are coming with the stuff Sir!", he is telling with excitement that the police team is arriving at the right time.

Tip off helpers like him, have been engaged by the Police all over the city. With each haul of stuff, whether caught at the Airport or at pubs, they get good cash rewards that are mostly unofficial.

****

CHAPTER TWO

Rahul woke up with the disturbing ringtone of his mobile.

It is 8.30 in the morning.

He reached the mobile which is ringing in his pants pocket and dared to disturb him with its vibration.

It is Imran.

"Imran, what's the matter?" he asked in a hoarse voice.

He could not open his eyes as he still feels the sleepiness. He knows that now there would be a lengthy class from Imran as he lost the job and he needs to give an explanation on how he lost the job and gets ready for consolation from Imran. He is really vexed with the repetition of the same thing very often. But he cannot avoid it to happen. Now too, as Imran contacted him, he is getting ready for the boring narration of the incident. Rahul yawned with irritation as he wished to sleep some more time because there would be nothing to do today.

"Happy New Year, *Yaar*!, I've been trying since last night....where are you?", Imran's voice is probing.

"Damn with the New Year... I lost my job....that son-of-a bitch...fatty buffalo... shunted me out...I returned to room last night", Rahul replied with the rising anger in his voice.

His anguish has brought him fully out of the sleepiness.

"What!?...Oh my God!! What happened?", Imran's voice is filled with concern and surprise.

Though Imran is well accustomed to face such conversations from Rahul whenever he loses a job, every time the worry haunts him as to how Rahul would be going to get a new job and how long it would take to find a new job. Till then the burden of looking after him falls on Imran.

"Tell me Yaar! What happened?", Imran repeated as Rahul was silent for a while.

"That bastard....Mallesh, that rascal.... got me fixed in the cash counter!", the anger mixed with pain is raising Rahul's voice to high pitch.

Imran could hear the fuming sound over phone.

"Oh! You did it again! Are you mad to repeat such mistakes again and again?...Come on, *Yaar*, what's this? Why don't you change this attitude?...How long would you be like this?...How painful it would be to hear such a bad news on New Year's Day? ", Imran yelled with a bit of anger in his voice.

It is not new for Imran to feel and get annoyed over the reckless attitude of Rahul in dealing with cash or even attending his the work assigned to him. Imran has made it a habit of warning Rahul frequently over the job he is doing. He knows very well that Rahul cannot survive on a particular job even for a quarter of the year.

Rahul waited a moment before starting his narration of what happened at his work site.

"That bastard told me to handle the billing since the lunch break.... by the evening.... there was a difference in the cash total in the counter system.... it was nearly seven thousands.....that rogue...Rajesh...cheated me while handing over the counter.... I was damn foolishly careless....Mallesh...Rascal... started shouting and made a big scene....that bastard spoke to the Chief Manager of the Mall.... threatened me...about making a complaint to police...it's all pre-planned....he is after that monkey faced bitch.....Rani.....now he got her in my place", Rahul's voice was curt and manifesting his disgust over the incident.

He gets a lot of relief whenever he chides and blame on others whom he consider as his enemies or those who cheated him.

Imran gave a patient hearing. He was silent for a few seconds and responded.

"Sorry...*Yaar!* .....What's the idea now?", Imran's voice turned thoughtful.

"I don't know", His voice is blank as if it is not his concern.

"Okay, you can find something else...leave it....you come to *The Heaven* by twelve thirty.... I'll be waiting.....we'll enjoy biryani there....and ...hey, it's also your birthday!....forgot?...I think you turned twenty seven...right?', Imran is trying to cheer up him.

"To hell with the birthday!... I don't have money....lost the job without payment", Rahul's voice turned harsh again.

"Come on...*Yaar!* I'll see that...don't forget", Imran knows how to console and how to get him cooled up.

He has been watching his moods since their teenage.

"Okay", Rahul switched off the mobile and lit the last cigarette found in his pocket.

After a couple of puffs, it struck to his mind that how much money was left with him.

He opened his worn-out purse. There is nothing more than seven hundred rupees and some change. He threw the purse aside. He turned gloomy and has started thinking of what to do now after having lost the latest of the innumerous jobs he had been hired and fired so far.

He had given up counting the serial number long back. But, the latest job loss is pinching because, he was cleverly got fixed in and shunted out without last payment.

'That bastard was cruel....really made a scene. He shoved, pushed and slapped me. All along entire staff were silent and unconcerned as if it was a routine matter. That bitch, Rani, made an innocent face!', Rahul's anger is not getting subsided while recollecting the course of incident happened to him at the Mall.

Really he was shocked and could not understand what was going on without his involvement.

"Bastards! Nobody was good at heart', he frowned throwing the butt of the cigarette to a corner of the room.

He is getting a sickening and burning feeling inside.

'I'm a fool, unfit to continue in any job....don't know how to lead a life...everybody is cheating me... wherever I work, I would be readily available for being easily trapped and cheated!', he felt a gushing emotion was trying to come out from the heart.

Suddenly, he came out of his emotions. Someone is gently tapping the door.

He looked at his mobile.

It is around 9.15 AM.

'Who is that at this time?', the sweeping maid wouldn't come so early...then who is that?', he felt surprised as the door is still being tapped slowly.

He shook his head and got up to open the door.

It is Sheela.

He was surprised on seeing her standing in front of him at his room.

'Why did she come here now!?', he was puzzled.

Generally, the residents of lower flats come over to the roof for hanging the washed clothes particularly, to hang thicker and heavy clothes or blankets on the steel wires that were fixed in four rows from one end of the roof to another end. He rarely see them as he wakes up and comes out of his room at around ten thirty in the mornings as most of his duties fall at second shifts late into nights.

She is the only daughter of one of the tenants in the second floor of the building. Rahul did not know much about her. As far as he knew, she has done a software engineering degree and is doing post-graduation in some Psychology related specialization courses in a top Institution.

Her father is an ordinary clerical level employee in a private company which fetches him just enough to wade through the flow of life that is nothing but full of never ending financial hardships. With the lower middle class mindset, her father is worrying of her marriage after completion of her graduation. But, now she is doing masters in a different stream and also interested in pursuing further education and ambitious of doing something in research side too. To meet her study expenses which her father is no longer able to meet, she is doing a part time job in the week ends teaching software skills to students in a school. Her father is not able to understand what and why she is still studying. But one thing he surely knows that she is so intelligent and smart enough to get good scores in each class since her childhood. Her mother wants her daughter to get an IT job so that it would be easier for them to get her married to a good looking software employee. Rahul gets so embarrassed whenever he has to confront with her while coming or going out from his room.

Now, that same young girl is standing in front of the door dressed up in a bright sky blue coloured *kurta* and black leggings. Her big and black eyes are glowing on seeing him.

"Happy New Year, Rahul!", she wished him with a graceful smile putting in his hand a piece of cake wrapped in paper cover.

Her soft and sweet refreshing voice is turning the ambience gloomy to cheerful. The new dress is well suited to her slim physique and the slight makeup enhanced her pretty looks in the morning sunlight that brightened her fair complexion too. A careful glance at her could reveal that she has taken enough care of her appearance before coming here.

"I lost my job", he replied as if that is the response to the New Year wishes.

"Oh my God! What a news on the very first day of the new year?, I am so... sorry, Rahul, you see... I didn't know!. Really sorry to know this!', her big eyes could reflect her genuine expressions along with her thin lips which could curl in tune to the sounds uttered.

He is silent, not knowing how to react. He is looking down as he could not see into her eyes. He does not know what to do when she offered a piece of cake on the very morning of a New Year Day. He looked at the cake in his hand for a while. It's a chocolate cake. She is looking at his straight nose and the unshaven cheeks while he is diverting his eyes towards sides. She never had such an opportunity to look and examine him standing so close to him that too when he is standing there motionless like a statue and hanging down his head looking at the floor.

'His eyes are also big!', she thought.

He seemed just got up from bed after a sound sleep without changing into causals. His curly and bushy hair is undone and the badly crumpled shirt is already got pulled off the sides of Jeans.

Standing so close to his tall body and looking up into his face is giving her a new sense of revelation of something out of a bunch of uncomprehending thoughts.

"What are you going to do now?", her eyes were filled with concern.

She had to speak again as she knows that he would not respond beyond a point of time for such embarrassing questions.

"Don't know, may be... I'll start searching for something else....I'm going out now", he tried to move backwards exhibiting his embarrassment.

She turned back and moved heavily towards downstairs. After a few steps, she looked back.

"Then...what about your room rent?... mom said... house owner rang up last night... and from this month....he has hiked the rent by one thousand rupees for all of us in the second floor and...five hundred for you... try for something... Rahul', she turned and went down stairs quickly.

He closed the door and moved towards bath room.

****

CHAPTER THREE

"Well done, Vinay! Come in...I'm happy.....you have caught these drug traffickers with the stuff...sit down", ACP Bhargav offered chair to Inspector Vinay Kumar, who with his team, had luckily stumbled upon a group of drug traffickers and buyers during his patrolling last night and caught them with sufficient quantity of heroin. Bhargav, is a young and sincere IPS officer and who has got a name to be reckoned with in solving tough cases. He got into fame with his relentless efforts and dedication in nabbing serial killers recently. Several murder cases, mafia cases including drug and human trafficking cases have been dealt by him with good results. As he is too keen to utilise human resources with high end technology to optimum level, his success rate is very high when compared to his peers in the department.

"Thank you Sir", Vinay Kumar saluted him stiffly before sitting down in the chair. He felt proud as the ACP complimented him in the presence of his team.

Sub-Inspector Raghu and two constables stood stiffly behind him. All their faces seemed beaming with the achievement on the very first day of the New Year.

Vinay Kumar carefully pulled out a plastic cover from the zip bag handed over by Sub-Inspector Raghu. He opened the cover and spread the contents onto the table.

"These are the small covers...in which the drug is sold Sir, ... very small quantity in each cover, Sir, We had seen

Pan masala sachets like covers and candy type forms too in our previous raids Sir...this time they experimented this way....in a cone form!", he showed a centimeter sized tiny packets made of water proof white paper in which the drug powder is packaged tightly by twisting all corners of the paper into one side which gives it a look of a cone.

"So...this is heroin?...at what rate these guys are selling it?", ACP Bhargav queried looking keenly into the white powder from an opened cone.

"One piece for two thousand rupees Sir!.... and it depends on the demand!...it may rise depending on the occasion! Sometimes, it's said, it may reach to four thousands too!.....we've seized sixty three covers in total... it's a good haul Sir!... we could catch hold of four persons Sir!...another two fellows escaped on seeing us... but we got the information fully from these fellows, Sir!", Vinay Kumar explained enthusiastically, pointing out his finger towards four youngsters standing in a row near to the wall, with their heads hanging down.

The youngsters are in their early twenties wearing casuals and with desperate looks in their faces for being caught on New Year Day.

Two of them are standing separately. They are apparently from rich family back grounds. The other two looked like road side small vendors.

ACP Bhargav interacted with the persons standing there in interrogative style. He seemed satisfied while nodding his head in tune to the running description given by Vinay Kumar. Once the ACP nodded his head finally, the youngsters were sent back to their cell.

"They got this stuff from Mumbai...Sir....but they are telling that they are retailers... the original smugglers who brought this into the country were not known to them....it's coming from some black youth...whose whereabouts are not known except mobile numbers...we got two numbers...but rascals... already got the smell.... must have changed the SIM cards, Sir", Vinay Kumar continued his narration.

"Okay Vinay!...try to corroborate it with the data and old info we're having on this case....we can come to a conclusion as to ensure whether the mafia behind this is the same or whether others also have entered the field afresh.... you know!, ...As the info we have got so far, some black youth who came here on the plea of pursuing higher studies are playing key role in supply and distribution of the stuff in the city...your team has already got some information on that...keep trying on that angle....And as far as this fellows who were caught now are concerned.....get ready all the paper work.....And before taking them to court, get them ready for the press meet....at Three O'clock....in the meanwhile, submit all the details for the case file...I'm going to meet the Commissioner to give a presentation on the case.... And you have done a good job!.. Your team deserves a cash award!", ACP Bhargav got up concluding the enquiry session.

"Thank you Sir...we will be ready Sir", Inspector Vinay Kumar got up with a broad beaming smile in his face and saluted the ACP standing stiffly like a rock statue.

The constables also followed him thudding their boots on the floor with a big noise in chorus.

****

"Actually...that Mall job doesn't suit to your mentality *Yaar* ...you did the right thing in losing it!", Imran declared his opinion rather seriously while transferring the spicy chicken leg piece into Rahul's plate.

"Enough", Rahul tried to obstruct the transfer in vain and concentrated on tasting the delicious and steaming Chicken Biryani.

New Year's first afternoon turned *The Heaven,* the famous biryani restaurant of this corner of the city, into a fish market with the turnout of a heavy crowd. Customers are impatiently yelling over the delay in getting the items ordered. The restaurant is abuzz with the service boys running on their toes, with the customers who are waiting at the reception for their turn and with the customers who have finished the lunch and coming out in groups, picking their teeth with tooth picks. The air is filled with the smell of steaming biryanis and kebabs. It took two hours for them to have sumptuous lunch ordering all the favourite items which Rahul would fondly eat.

"So....what's the idea now?", Imran came to the point after coming out of the restaurant.

They stood at the pan shop adjacent to the restaurant under a tree. Imran ordered two sweet pan. After having Biryani there, Imran would like to taste a sweet pan.

'I'm thinking...nothing is striking', Rahul replied lighting a cigarette offered by Imran.

'By the way,....I forgot to tell you...*Yaar*... you know Mastan's cousin!,,, that who's residing in Mumbai?...I told you know...Riyaz?...when he had worked here three years ago,.... he used to appreciate my work very often.... remember him?....now, he is forcing me to come over to Mumbai...he has recently opened a tailoring shop there...he wants me to join him.'

'Are you going to Mumbai?', Rahul asked with surprise in his voice.

After maintaining silence for few seconds, Imran responded.

'See *Yaar!*.....I'm a tailor...what else can I do?... here...that Mastan Sahib is not paying me much...we're not earning much to save anything...what we get is enough for meeting the ends!....We've already come of age and grown up.... When to settle down in the life?... and... unlike you,... I know nothing else....and this opportunity appears to be fine...Riyaz offered me one third of daily earnings....you know how would be the rates in Mumbai? That's more than enough for a comfortable living in Mumbai....isn't it?', Imran is in a defensive mood.

'When will you leave?', Rahul asked him, while thinking on the side lines of his mind that what stopped him from not having tried tailoring so far.

'Tomorrow evening....I couldn't get train reservation....going by bus....I got sleeper ticket....you know....it's more than twelve hours...overnight journey!', Imran's voice is reflecting boyish joy over his journey in search of a new livelihood.

Suddenly, he stopped for a second and looked into Rahul's eyes as Rahul was looking somewhere.

'Would you like to come over there?... I hope...you would get a job in Mumbai that would suit to you...you can start a new life there!....what do you say?', Imran asked him with an expression in his eyes expecting a positive response from him.

Rahul is silent.

'You think *Yaar*...you've not been successful here....I know you can do many things... ...Mumbai is much bigger than this...opportunities are more... you know?' Imran is trying to project a positive picture about the future.

Rahul is thinking deeply puffing the cigarette.

'Okay....you think slowly...take a decision...I'm going there...once I settled down there...you can join me...and....sorry for leaving you like this....I'll find something for you *Yaar*...don't worry....Right?' Imran concluded with some soothing consolation in his voice.

Before taking leave, Imran stopped for a moment and searched in his pocket for something. His hand came out with a few folded currency notes.

'Keep this...Three thousands...I can't give much....you know...I have to take care of initial expenses at Mumbai', Imran dabbed the money into Rahul's pocket.

'I'll return this once I got a job', thankful relief appeared in Rahul's eyes.

'No hurry Yaar...first try to find something', Imran tried to be adamant.

"I'm badly in need of money....actually I have to pay room rent today...that Sheela told me...owner hiked it from this month", Rahul's voice is turning soft.

"Sheela?...Oh...that Second floor girl?...she is pretty with big eyes Yaar...these days she is talking to you often....you know...you are tall and handsome ....what's the matter?", Imran pretended diverting the topic.

'Will you shut up your mouth?...I'm not interested in such things...we...poverty ridden beggars...shouldn't indulge in such extra things!", Rahul's voice turned angry.

'Okay...okay...Yaar...don't get angry with me...that day you saved her from those bastards...perhaps...she may be a bit thankful to you...and nothing else...is it okay now?' Imran is playful again.

'I didn't go there to save her...till then I didn't know who she was... I was traveling in the same compartment at that time...it could happen to any girl....anybody could come forward to rescue...it was incidental...that's all...see...she is...I think...studying some PG course in a famous college"...she is a good girl...from a decent family background...we should not think of such girls', Rahul tried to correct the scene.

'Seems...more information's been gathered about her....okay...okay...Yaar...I'll stop now', Imran laughed raising his hands across his face as if protecting from the stern looks of Rahul.

'Okay...let's go now...give me a ring...I'll come to the bus station tomorrow...see you', Rahul shook his hand and turned back.

Imran stood there for a while watching Rahul walking to the nearby bus stop.

'Good guy...but bad times!', he sighed and moved towards the stands where he parked his old bicycle.

****

CHAPTER FOUR

Sheela is sitting in the balcony of her flat. Suddenly she heard the sound of footsteps. She became attentive.

'Rahul is going down!' she confirmed herself.

She stood up and started looking down from her balcony. After a few minutes, Rahul appeared coming down from stair case of the building and started walking along the by-lane towards the main road. She kept watching him from behind.

He appeared dull and is engrossed in deep thinking. His tall body is now slogging with his head bowing down projecting him a loser leaving the field.

She watched him till he turned from the corner of the by-lane and disappeared from her sight.

She sighed heavily.

'Poor guy!...leading a troubled life...lost his source of income...he should get a suitable job very soon' , she prayed to god for bestowing him with grace.

Suddenly, she got struck with the memory of that day! She got a jerk all over her body.

'What a day it was?', she felt the shiver again. Still, she is inclined to hover over the experience of the hateful night of her life that is often attacking her with disturbing night-mares.

'What a worst day in my life!', she whispered to herself.

That day, three months ago, she was returning to the city after attending a wedding function of her close friend cum classmate at a major town located at a distance of more than hundred kilometers. Though her mother worried over her traveling alone out of the city such a long distance, Sheela convinced her that she would return by evening at least by Seven O'clock. But, as the function was delayed and run into the evening, Sheela worried to leave for the city as soon as possible.

Though her friend insisted her to stay back that night, Sheela did not agree as she had promised her mother that she would return without much delay.

Generally, she prefers bus journey. But because of the proximity to the railway station, her friend suggested train journey because she could reach home before it becomes too late in the night.

Declining her friend's suggestion that her cousin would accompany her up to City Railway Station, Sheela went to the nearby railway station alone and caught the seven thirty local passenger train.

After informing her mother that she was coming by the local train, her mobile got switched off as it was out of power. Sheela cursed herself for not having charged her phone at the function hall. It needed urgent power charging. As the charging points were not working in the train, she could not get her mobile charged.

The passenger crowd in the General compartment she got in was thin. She went inside and sat on a window seat nearer to some female commuters. She felt comfortable and when the train moved, she started thinking about the funny things she shared with other classmates who attended the function. The train, being a local shuttle service, was having halts for every now and then. Though one and a half hours passed, the train had not moved much towards the destination.

Suddenly, she came out of her thoughts as a hand touched her shoulder from behind. She quickly looked that side with shock filled eyes. Somebody sitting back side stretched his hand and started to rub her shoulder.

She pushed away the hand with rising anger and looked around. There were no female passengers in the nearby seats except two guys in early twenties sitting in front of her who were chuckling while their eyes were freely engaged in thorough scanning of her body.

She got chills in her spine.

Cursing herself for getting immersed in thoughts and not observing what is happening around her, she stood up and moved to sit along with some others. Much to her bewilderment, she found none in the compartment.

It is empty.

She went up to the door. Two more similar guys are standing there and looking towards her with the same chuckling smiles.

This is new to her!

She has never faced such a situation!

She sensed that she is shivering. She realized the danger she fell in.

As the train is in full motion and there is no connection through the compartments, she is not able to do anything for escaping from them.

She got some courage on thinking that some station would come hopefully within a few minutes, so that she could change into next compartment.

She moved towards other side of the compartment.

The two guys who were sitting in front of her already stood up and came so close to her.

“Move aside”, she said seriously.

They moved aside giving way to her.

She walked towards the other door.

But, the person who put his hand on her shoulder is now standing across her way and holding the seats on both sides to make her understand that she cannot move further.

“Let us sit down.....why standing so long?” he is smiling mischievously.

He is in early thirties and looks like a street vendor. He seems the leader of the gang. He came closer to her.

She felt some strong and unbearably pungent smell. He is chewing something like a pan masala.

She moved back. But, the others are also standing so close to her.

In all, they are five.

“What is this?....what do you think?....I will sit somewhere, leave me alone!”, she raised her voice making them to know that she is tough and serious.

“Why are you shouting?...none can listen....station is far away....let us sit down.”, the leader’s voice turned hard.

Now it is clear for her that they are really ready for doing something more than just teasing.

Suddenly, she moved towards the window side to pull the chain yelling as much bigger as she could, “Help...Help!...”.

The leader pushed her onto a berth and covered her mouth with his hand.

As she was trying hard to remove his hand, he held and pressed her body to the berth.

Others flocked around and held her feet and hands.

She is frantically trying to get up and remove herself from their grip.

The leader put his hand around her neck and is trying to tear off her dress.

Suddenly, he was thrown back as if someone pulled from behind.

Others got up and looked back.

As the grip got loosened, Sheela tried to see what is happening.

One tall and strong young man is holding the hair and shirt of the leader from behind.

He looked very serious or rather furious while dragging him to the door. He quickly banged the head of the leader to the window and threw him out of the door.

The other gang members are looking bewildered with what is happening before them.

It took a few seconds for them to realize that someone suddenly came and threw their leader out of the compartment.

As the train is in full speed, they couldn't hear his yells while being thrown out. They are not sure whether their leader was dead or alive with injuries.

Before they are coming out of the shock, the young man held one more person and punched him in the face and banged his head to a side seat while kicking hard one more person below the stomach at the same time.

The first person fell unconscious and the second one knelt down badly moaning with pain. The young man kicked the second person one more time on his head.

He dragged the first person towards the door and pushed him out of compartment. He was so quick and moving methodically while attacking them.

The other two members of the gang were frightened as two of them were thrown out of the compartment. One of them suddenly brandished a knife from his pocket.

But, the young man didn't give him much scope. He kicked him so hard on his chest that he flew in air a foot up and fell back a few feet away on hitting an aisle seat.

As the young man moved towards him menacingly, he quickly got up and ran towards the door and jumped out of the compartment.

He moved back towards the other person, a teenager. He folded his hands praying not to beat him. But the young man is so furious that he kicked him towards the door.

The teenager got up and jumped out of the compartment.

Train slowed down as it is approaching a station.

He looked from the window.

It is the last and destination station for the train where he has to get down.

He looked around.

The person who was hit on below his belly got up and quickly stepped out onto the platform.

The young man looked towards Sheela.

Sheela is shivering while witnessing the uncomprehending flow of action taking place before her eyes. She wondered how the young man came into the train. She thought that he must have been in the back side of the compartment.

"Are you Okay?", he asked coming nearer to her.

Sheela nodded her head.

"Okay... let's get down. Station has arrived.", He told.

Sheela stood up and took her bag and upper cloth and got down behind him.

Though still in shock, she could recognize him. He is a tenant in the top floor of the building where she is residing. But, she is not sure whether he has recognized her.

"Can you go home alone?", He enquired her.

She got it confirmed that he didn't recognize her.

"I am Sheela... we are in the second floor of the building where you reside" She told without rising her head.

Her voice is hoarse and could not hide the shiver.

"Oh!..", it is surprising for him that he has beaten blue and black some persons who had tried to molest a young girl residing in the same building.

He looked into her face. He has never seen her earlier.

She is looking down. Her lips are dried. Hair looks roughly undone in the tussle. She is fair and tall and must be in her early twenties.

"Okay let's go", he said moving his eyes as she rose her eyes.

Sheela followed him. She knew him. She had seen him several times while coming or going into their building. She observed him as the most unconcerned person as if he was not related to this area or had come from some other place as a guest. He appeared as an odd man out in the premises. He was always seen walking with a serious face that always kept bowing down. She observed him moving as if he was in a trance.

Twice she had seen him smoking outside the building premises.

'Today I have seen a new person in him!', Sheela thought walking behind him.

She could not believe that a single person beating four or five persons without giving any scope to them to retaliate. She could watch such scenes in movies only which she used to think baffling. Now she saw that became a reality in her presence.

Both were silent till reaching the residential building. It's already 10 PM. They entered the building premises.

"Your name?," Suddenly, Sheela came forward and asked him.

"I'm.....I'm.... Rahul....living in the room on the roof", though fumbled a bit at the unexpected question, he replied as a matter of fact.

"Thanks Rahul", she told him with folded hands.

Her voice is still hoarse and eyes are wet. Her big eyes are straight and well expressing her feel of gratitude.

She set right her hair and wiped her face with the upper cloth and moved quickly towards the stair case. While hurriedly walking towards her flat, Sheela looked down.

She saw him lighting a cigarette standing nearer the entrance of the building.

"What are you doing there? ..... Come inside......Lunch is ready", Sheela came into the present with her mother's voice.

She looked around.

It's already 1.30 PM.

She heaved a sigh with a feeling of satisfaction in recollecting the incident of that night.

She moved into her flat.

****

CHAPTER FIVE

Rahul went around the City till the evening.

He met old masters who had hired him earlier and also tried new areas-computer institutes, internet cafes, automobile shops, restaurants, corporate hospitals and private colleges. Nothing seemed prospective.

He was surprised as to why the city had changed into a fully occupied place for each and every kind of jobs.

Though got an offer in a corporate hospital as a security staff, the salary offered was very low. It would be sufficient to pay rent of his room. It is not quite affordable for him to live separately in a residential block.

But he chose the present accommodation most suitable since it is giving him the needed seclusion and privacy in a family atmosphere and hence he is not ready to vacate it though rent is on higher side. And though he does not like to interact with his neighbours, he always likes to reside at sort of a family residential locality. He needs a job that can meet at least all the basic requirements including the rent.

Finally, he decided to try at pubs. Earlier also he had worked at a couple of pubs.

'These young fellows are getting crazy about hanging around there...and more pubs are mushrooming in and around posh localities and also in outskirts where these people find fun and enjoyment in a secluded atmosphere, yes... that would be my next target', He thought.

On getting down from a city bus at City Station, he entered into Omega Hotel and got a cup of Irani tea.

While he is tastefully sipping its jaggery like sweetness, a hand firmly touched his shoulder from behind along with an unfamiliar voice with a different accent saying "Hi...friend!".

Rahul looked back surprising with the unexpected touch and voice.

He saw a young African grinning with a wide mouth and looking into his eyes as if he has known him from ages.

Rahul looked puzzled. He has never been friends with foreigners.

"You are working in Super Mall...aren't you?", asked the African as an introduction to further talk.

"Not any more", Rahul replied with probing eyes.

Wearing casual maroon coloured T-shirt and dark blue Jeans, the African young man is strong and equal in height and seems about of the same age.

Inspite of his simple appearance, his attire indicates that he is not so. The T-shirt appears to be costly.

Though Rahul is trying hard, nothing is striking to his mind to give any hint about this foreigner.

"Yeah...I knew that... they've shunted you...in fact, they were very cruel to you...insulted you.....Didn't they cheat you?', African continued with a sympathetic expression in his face.

"I don't know who you are!...How do you know about that?", Rahul asked still struggling with a puzzled state of mind.

"See...I'm your friend...your well-wisher!...I saw the entire scene there!...let's go to some restaurant so that we can speak out our minds...come with me...believe me friend!", he took Rahul's hand and gently dragged him out of the Hotel like an old friend.

"About what?", Rahul questioned him, though stepping out along with him.

"I'll tell you my friend, come with me", he moved forward leading to a nearby family restaurant.

It's an old fashioned eating place, still running for those old timers who are fondly accustomed to olden-days habits and atmosphere. The business is dull. The African led him to a corner table.

He ordered for *Puri* and coffee.

And after sending off the waiter, he got to the business with Rahul.

"I'm Jack,....Jackson...You can call me Jack....All my friends call me so...", he offered his hand towards Rahul.

Rahul did not move his hand.

"What's the matter? Why we are here?....Come to the point" , Rahul is never cordial with strangers.

"See....friend...you need not be scared of me or suspicious of me. I told you...know?...I'm your well-wisher...I've brought you here... just to help you... isn't it?" , he stopped for a while as the waiter brought the plates.

Rahul is careful in listening and catching his accent.

"Let's talk over the snacks...come on friend...don't treat me like a stranger", he pushed a plate towards Rahul and started eating from his own.

'What type of help I can expect from you?', Rahul asked him without touching the hot *Puri* in the plate. Actually, he is hungry and the hot *Puri and Kurma* is tempting him.

"You're fired...shunted out...I know you are a sincere hard worker...I believe such a person shouldn't be victimized...that's why I've come forward to help you...I'll see that you'll get a fine and well fetching job that'll put you in a better position!...got it? Now start eating...the Puri would get cold!', he stopped a while to gulf down *Kurma* filled *Puri*, with a glass of water.

"So you want to offer me some job?...what's that any way?", Rahul's voice is a bit soft now. He started to eat the *Puri*. It's really tasty.

"Yes...you got the point straight...you'll get a job...that really suits to you...you'll get good money out of it...we need persons like you...you see...I've been on this searching task for quite some time...luckily I got you...I observed the entire thing happened in the Mall", he finished eating and started to sip the hot coffee.

"You've not yet told me what the job is!", Rahul took the coffee cup and started sipping it with some hope slowly rising in his mind along with the steam coming out of the cup.

Jack laughed and looked into Rahul's eyes, "Do you think you'll get whatever the job you want?....by the way...what type of job you would like to do...I say?", his tone is turning a little bit instigating.

Everything in his face is big. His nose, eyes and mouth, all are big ...Rahul is thinking while staring into his face.

"Yes...I can do anything....but I need to know what that would be", he is curt a little bit.

It is interesting now. He finished the coffee.

"Let's move out", Jack paid the bill and got up leaving the remaining change as tip to the waiter.

Both came out of the restaurant and started walking. Rahul's appetite has been satiated. He is following him thoughtfully.

Jack stopped under a tree and looked around as if to ensure that nobody is watching them.

"The job is easy....but requires reliable persons", Jack lit a cigarette.

He stopped for a while.

"Would you be reliable?", he looked into Rahul's eyes.

"You told...that suits to me", Rahul replied lighting the cigarette offered by him.

"Yes...again you got the point straight! Yes, it does! It...is...too risky...but...would fetch good money too!", he smoked deeply looking sideways.

Now his face is a bit relaxed and with signs of enthusiasm as a result of the changed course of conversation from other side.

Rahul is silent.

Something is fishy...he is thinking.

Jack looked around.

On confirming that no one is observing, he casually pulled out of his pocket a small pouch.

It is a popular brand *Pan Masala* pouch that is available at any road side *Pan Shop*.

'This is the stuff...you will have to hand over it to the parties ordered for it...and collect the money from them and transfer it to me after deducting your commission', he stopped a while for Rahul's reaction.

"It's a *Pan Masala* Packet!...isn't it...then...why? What's so confidential and secret about it?", Rahul asked him while his mind is turning suspicious.

"Yes...you are right my friend...it's a *pan masala* pouch...Yes,....but....inside it,...what's the stuff...you know?....It's h-e-r-o-i-n!!..........yes.......heroin...that's why it is secret...that's why it is risky....but this is the best way to get the stuff to change hands safely...you know?", his voice is low and husky though very clear.

He is stressing each word as if to emphasize each bit of his speech.

Rahul touched the packet. Slowly, slight shivering started in his back.

It is a small packet.

But instead of usual granules of *pan masala*, his hand sensed some soft powdery content inside it.

He felt chilled as if something is going down his spine. His eyes are wide. He is looking into Jack's eyes.

H-e-r-o-i-n!

He heard about it.

'The Police are after it. I watched on the TV many times about the rising drug trafficking menace in the City...and now I am standing in front of one such a fellow!...that too...with an unknown foreigner!', Rahul is thinking as his mind is filled with fear of this strange situation that is not leading him to any conclusion.

"That's it my friend...I observed you closely...after watching you several days...I got faith in you...we need most reliable persons....Ours is a big network.....need not worry and don't get scared of anybody...I firmly believe that it suits to you and ...you can handle it safely...and...listen....for handing over each packet...you would get one-thousand-rupees...it's big money...isn't it?", Jack stopped for a while and put the pouch inside his pocket looking around to ensure that none is observing them.

"It's risky!", Rahul said with his mouth turning dry.

He is suddenly getting thirsty.

"Yes...I've already told you know?....that's why...the big commission...one thousand rupees per a pouch!", Jack is stressing each word again.

"How much it costs?", Rahul's voice turned meek.

"This is a five thousand rupees pouch...so...you would get twenty percent commission...that's not small!...isn't it?", Jack's voice turned husky again with a look in his eyes with an indication that he got him already dragged half way through the deal.

Rahul is silent.

"See...friend..Ra...what's that...I forgot your name...is it....", Jack fumbled a bit trying to remember his name.

"I'm Rakesh", Rahul now got the confirmation that this African guy is playing tricks not knowing fully about him.

"Yes that's Rakesh!...Nice!.Okay...Rakesh...think and take a decision!...so far you have led a life like a daily wage labour...isn't it?....you've led life so ordinarily...you were always...short of money. You have put all your energies, strain...effort,...your sweat, everything...into your job....but what they paid was paltry...wasn't that?.....now opportunity is waiting before you...if you are ready...your life would be different...big money...new way of life...think friend...make a call to this number by ten thirty tonight... if you are ready to do this job...say yes...keep it as a top secret...otherwise both would be in danger...Okay?" he put a piece of paper in Rahul's hand and quickly moved away without looking back.

Rahul is looking towards him.

Jack is walking fast but appeared to be casual. Soon he joined the crowd on the foot path and disappeared from his sight.

It took him quite some time to come out of the unexpected and bewildering situation.

****

CHAPTER SIX

Rahul is standing with his body leaning on to the railing of Lake Road abutting the City Lake.

Unlike the big statue that is standing in an assuring posture on a big rock in the midst of the lake, his mind is not giving him any confidence.

After Jack's departure, he came here in a city bus.

He looked into the murky waters of the famous Lake that is dividing the city into two parts. Along the Lake Road and around the Lake, all the roads are illuminated with street lights.

The traffic is heavy.

Passersby and those who came for a relaxed evening at Lake Road are slowly leaving for homes.

Still the area is alive and abuzz.

But his mind is oscillating. Jack's words are ringing in his ears.

What to do?

Whether to accept Jack's proposal or to say no?

What would be better and safe?

This is really risky.

This is nothing but inviting the trouble into my life, that's already been in shambles.

But how it would be if he takes necessary precautions?

He is searching for suitable answers from his mind.

Though being a victim of ever haunting hardships, he never indulged into such unlawful activities.

What to do?

Nothing is coming to his mind. It's lingering in dilemma like the dark and murky waters of the Lake.

He is thinking as his mind is getting blank and is not indicating any hopeful idea of what to do now.

Imran had left for Mumbai two days ago. Otherwise, he would have approached him for a solution to this problem.

His mind slowly went into deep memories towards his childhood.

He is not holding any patch of memory that could portray a clear picture of his childhood life. His track of memory starts with himself being ten years old boy.

He was brought up in his uncle's house in a poor atmosphere in a semi urban village area about a hundred kilometres away from the city. His uncle, who was a distant relation from his father's side, used to tell him that he was born on January first day in a neighbouring village where his mother, an innocent and beautiful village girl, died of some viral fever a couple of months after his birth.

His father left her after a few months of marital life and thereafter his whereabouts were not known. He was said to have been killed in a series of bomb explosions took place in the forest area where there were clashes between police and Maoists. Many villagers who helped either Maoists or police were said to have been killed in the explosions or in the encounters. As per his uncle's un-clarified version, his father belonged to a higher community while his mother was a *Dalit*.

He cursed himself many times for losing the basic birth right of seeing the faces of his parents.

While he was studying elementary education in a local school, his uncle was killed in a train accident that took place at a nearby railway station.

Afterwards, life turned miserable. His uncle's widow left for her native place leaving him as an orphan. The old small hut with palm leaves roof where his uncle resided till his death had now slowly got dilapidated due to lack of proper maintenance. Despite of rains and cold, he had led life taking shelter under it for a few years and there after abandoned it and started taking shelter in the verandah of the village community hall.

Neighbours were somewhat sympathetic over his fate and helped for his growth till he had completed school final. Though an orphan and poor, he was good at studies and came out successful in his school final examination with top grades in all subjects.

The village head gifted him with a pair of new clothes.

But loneliness had always haunted him.

Because of his poverty ridden background, he could not pursue higher studies. There after none of the villagers came forward to afford his livelihood or education. He was not interested in continuing higher studies.

Already his mind clarified him that he was different.

He used to glare at the children being pampered by their parents.

The feeling of being an orphan had hardened his mind and he developed a mindset that had always been far older than his actual age.

A small mirror in his uncle's house had been his only solace to talk to himself. Whenever he got that urge, he used to go to the mirror.

He used to find a small boy in the mirror with an unattractive face, thin cheeks and dull eyes reflecting poor looks.

He didn't like his face.

Everyone looked better except himself.

At his age, when all other children were indulged in playful and fun filled life, he used to think of where to get a handful of food and a few feet of shelter.

He was eager to help others in petty and miscellaneous works so that he would get food before going to sleep.

He used to sleep in the verandah of the village community hall for several years.

One day he left the place, with a firm mind that this village was not anymore suitable place for him to survive and hence, he should try a new life in the City.

He remembered that on January first ten years back, he landed in this city in search of a new life.

For the last ten years he had tried at many jobs.

He changed many places for shelter within the city.

Over the years, he got good knowledge of various jobs and skills.

He got license for driving heavy vehicles.

He knows computer operation and servicing.

He could speak, read and write three languages.

He worked as sales boy and salesman.

He tried as a mechanic, driver, peon and telephone operator.

He also tried as bar waiter, server, construction labour, toilet cleaner and many more.

But, he could not be successful in continuing in any one of them for more than a year.

His indifferent and unconcerned attitude always affected his job projecting him as an unreliable human being.

Nobody had shown a bit of affection during the course of livelihood.

He has been haunted with a feeling of loneliness.

Ten years!

Yes, ten years have passed over his struggle for a life that led him nowhere since he landed in the city.

Why people are not good at heart?

Why I've been unfit to win over the hearts or affection of the people I met so far?

I'm just meant for being cheated and shunted out from one place to another.

But, why it was so for me only?

That feeling of burning anger is growing again with an urge to do something to get himself cooled up.

Suddenly, Rahul came out of his ponderings and deep memory lanes.

A beggar is asking for some coins for tea.

He shook his head and stood up to move.

'Better to go to room', he decided.

***

Rahul reached his room.

Opened the door and sank into the bed. Though tired, he is not sleepy because his mind is struggling with the haunting thoughts. He could not eat anything except having several cups of tea as he lost the appetite to eat something. His mind is hovering around various conclusions but the issue is the same.

What to do?

It's already 10.30 PM.

He lit a cigarette in support of his pondering process. Since the morning he has been smoking a lot. He is feeling that an unknown force is urging him to take a decision. He is running out of money. He is left with a few hundreds and some change. If he spends that, he will have to look for money at least to satisfy the pangs of hunger from tomorrow.

What to do? Why a foreigner came into my life? Why I'm so disturbed after meeting this guy?

After struggling with so many ways and so many jobs to lead a life, now I'm left with a new job!....Drug delivery!?

Is it safe? Isn't it a crime?

He has never indulged in any criminal activities earlier though tried at many jobs for survival.

In fact, he could keep himself at a distance from crimes and criminal activities though he had faced such situations in some jobs where he worked.

Now this is risky!....It's a crime! Earning money by delivering prohibited stuff is something he has never imagined of. But it is fetching good money he had never earned in any of his earlier jobs. That is true!

What would be his position once he would be caught by police while delivering the stuff?

Would he be in jail?

Rahul is introspecting himself or rather, interrogating himself. His fingers are madly running through his hair and sometimes dragging the hair as if plucking it off.

Suddenly, he stood up and went to the mirror. He stood there staring at his reflection. He found a young man with poor looks. He didn't like his face. Thinned cheeks, blackened and sunken eyes that are lacking light, madly grown hair with a rough beard, leaned neck and sagging shoulders!

What a face is this?

Why should I be so?

Why am I alone?

What's wrong with me?

Why can't I be in a better position?

Why every damn rogue is able to cheat me?

Would I live and die like an unknown orphan for want of a job that gives me a comfortable and sure life?

Would it be so forever? Will it be so forever??

Suddenly, he covered his face in his hands.

He got an unexpected burst. He wept out with tears flowing down and wetting his palms. He felt lonely and helpless. His deep agony slowly turned into anger.

"No...not anymore!", he shouted out in anger.

"Yes...I must say yes to Jack!...Yes...that's the best answer to all my troubles! Why should I be afraid of all these buggers who are always after me? I should lead a life of my choice....I have a right to choose a job which could give me all the comforts of a joyful life!", he is speaking out to himself...rather, to his reflection in the mirror.

As he is still in a self-assuring mood that is successfully forcing his mind to yield to the inner urge, his mobile started ringing. He took the mobile into his hands.

It's Jack!

'How did he get my number? Rahul wondered.

By now, he got the confirmation that this guy had got all the information about him. He lifted the call.

"Yes Jack...I'm ready", his voice is firm and reflecting a changed tone.

****

CHAPTER SEVEN

Rahul arrived to his room.

It's already 11.30 PM.

He closed the door and sat down on his cot.

His mind was blank for a while.

Suddenly, he searched in his pocket.

He took out the cover from his pocket. It is stapled with pins. He tore off the cover at the top and took out the currency notes from it.

All are hundred rupees notes. He hurriedly counted them. He once again counted the notes to ensure whether the count was correct.

'Four thousand rupees for doing such a secret job!', Rahul felt excited as if he had achieved something extraordinary in a single day by earning that much money at a time. He has never earned so much money on any single day in his life.

He lit a cigarette and started to recollect the events took place since the morning.

He met Jack in the morning after waiting patiently for more than an hour at a point he told last night. Jack appeared serious. On approaching him, Jack did not stop there.

He simply whispered to follow him and proceeded towards other side of the road.

It is a slum locality with sparse movement of people. Jack took him to a by lane.

He handed over a small piece of paper roughly scribbling something. It is a mobile number.

"Contact this number...That person will give you the stuff...he will tell you where to hand over it...Must complete the task by 11.00 PM...Thereafter...You will get your payment...Okay?...By the way, your code name is number four....Be careful while on the job....Okay?...Got it?...You will get a message from this number whenever stuff arrives", Jack stopped telling while looking straight into his eyes.

Rahul has got a chill in the spine on hearing the narration. He simply nodded his head in response.

"Hereafter, I will not be seen unless it is compulsory", Jack concluded the instructions and left from there briskly.

Rahul waited there for a few minutes after Jack left to confirm that he was alone. He made a call to the mobile number.

"Number Four?", a curtly voice enquired.

"Yes...Four....Number Four...yes that is my number", Rahul confirmed with a fumbling voice.

"See the message and delete", the call cut off.

Rahul searched in his mobile.

Yes, there is a message! The meeting point and time mentioned in it. It is nothing but his favourite Omega Hotel where he likes Irani tea.

Now he has to meet someone at Omega Hotel at 12.00 PM.

He deleted the message and lit a cigarette.

'So they must have been observing me!', he thought.

He saw the time.

It is already 11.30 AM.

He came out of the by-lane and looked around to ensure that none was observing him. He called a nearby Auto.

"Omega Hotel", he told the driver adjusting himself into the middle of the seat.

****

Omega Hotel is abuzz with lunch time rush.

Rahul entered the Tea Section and took a cup of Irani tea.

He started to see around as to ensure who is that someone handing over the stuff to him.

"Don't look around...just keep sipping tea....CC Cameras are there", a voice came from behind.

Rahul wondered how that person had identified him.

'This must be a big network than what I expected!', he is thinking.

He finished his tea.

Suddenly, a person came close to him with a cup of tea.

Rahul looked at him.

He is a short man in his thirties wearing a green jerkin and blue jeans and a cap that is covering half of his face as he is looking down.

'He must be like me, he is not one of the main persons in the network', Rahul is thinking.

"A small bag is there below the wash basin..... Go and take it....that is the stuff bag......there is a slip with details of places and numbers where to handover it.....do it carefully", he finished looking somewhere.

Rahul heard attentively and looked towards wash basin.

Yes, there is a small bag!

"What's your name?....What about my payment?", Rahul enquired with excited voice.

"After completing the job....Payments are made by somebody...The details are also there in the slip....Don't worry....My name is...number three....most probably...you will be getting supply through me in future too...if not possible...someone will be engaged....Okay?, he smiled and moved out without looking at Rahul.

Rahul waited a minute there and reached the wash basin. He washed his hands and looked below the wash basin.

It is there.

He bent down wiping his hands with handkerchief and took the bag casually as if he had kept it there while washing hands. He pushed it into his pocket.

Rahul moved out after confirming that nobody was observing him. He reached a nearby street where movement is less. He searched in the bag. There is a plastic cover inside the bag containing four small packets.

The packets are just like some pan masala packets. None can think them containing heroin powder. He touched a packet.

He could sense that it is containing small amount of powder inside.

He saw a slip in the plastic cover.

He opened the slip.

Places and timings were scribbled in English. Downward arrow marks were given after each line of description.

First place is seven kilometers away.

Rahul should buy a cigarette at the *Pan shop* near the bus stop at 3.00 PM. He should drop a packet after finishing the cigarette.

The next place is around five kilometers from the first place where he should drop the second and third packets at 5.00 PM.

After finishing tea in the right corner table in the nearby restaurant, he should drop the packets below his table.

The third place is around ten kilometers from there. He should drop the last packet at 7.00 PM.

He saw the time in his mobile.

It is already 2.10 PM.

He threw away the bag and put the plastic cover inside his pocket. After coming out from the secluded street, he called an Auto.

****

Rahul reached the first place.

It is one of the eastern side areas of the City which has well expanded with the mushrooming IT companies. On getting down from the Auto near the bus stand, he slowly went to the nearby *Pan shop*. He bought a cigarette and lit it.

It is around 3.00 PM. He looked around.

A few people are standing in the bus stop waiting for buses. One young man is anxiously looking at him. Rahul looked at him keenly. He is in his early twenties and looks like a software employee in expensive attire.

On getting the eye contact, he slowly nodded his head. Rahul too nodded his head. On finishing the cigarette, Rahul slowly took out a packet from his pocket and dropped it on the floor. The young man quickly came to the Pan shop and asked the vendor for a cigarette. While lighting the cigarette, he bent down and took the packet from the floor.

'Thanks', he whispered and briskly moved from there.

Rahul looked around. None was observing the handing over process. He sighed in relief and saw the time.

It is around 3.15PM. He called an Auto.

****

It took more than an hour to reach the second place as the afternoon traffic was heavy. It is the north eastern part of the city.

The area is full of evening crowd.

Rahul looked around for the spot mentioned in the slip.

It is a small fast food point located at the right side of the road where he got down from the Auto.

He slowly went to the food point and stood beneath a small cloth roofing sheet arranged as sunshade.

The fast food selling point is full of customers eating evening snacks.

He went inside and ordered for samosas. He came out with samosa plate and sat down on a plastic chair under the roofing sheet.

Rahul once again looked around whether anyone is waiting for him. As nobody seemed waiting for him, he slowly started eating the samosas. The hot samosas are crunchy and tasty. As he has not taken anything since the morning, he felt hungry.

On finishing the last one, he threw away the paper plate and went inside for ordering tea. He came out with the plastic tea cup and stood again under the roofing sheet.

'Waiting for you for the last two hours', someone whispered from his back.

Rahul looked back.

A man aged around thirty years is standing behind him. He looked like an office assistant working in corporate companies.

'Why so late?', he whispered again in a complaining tone.

Rahul saw the time in his mobile.

It is 5.05 PM in the evening.

"I am at the right time", Rahul whispered back while putting his hand inside his pocket.

He doesn't like arguments.

He simply took out two packets from his pocket and dropped them on the floor.

The man, who is impatiently observing every small movement of Rahul, quickly bent down and picked up the two packets from the floor and went away from the spot within seconds.

'What a man of hurry?', Rahul sighed in relief as this task has also been finished.

He looked around and ensured that none was observing his packet transferring process.

He lit a cigarette and took out the slip to see the last spot.

***

Rahul looked in his mobile.

It was 7.30 PM.

He has been waiting for the last one hour near an Irani tea restaurant.

As per the slip, this is the last place where he should have a cup of tea and light a cigarette so that the receiver would come and collect the packet.

Rahul has already smoked three cigarettes.

He felt this procedure is somewhat boring as the receiver is yet to turn up.

He looked around to see whether anyone was watching and waiting for him.

The small restaurant is abuzz with evening crowd. Customers are busy in sipping tea and munching hot snacks like samosa and egg puffs.

Rahul felt hungry.

'Better to have something', he thought.

He raised his hand to call the waiter.

"Wait a minute", someone whispered from behind.

Rahul stopped calling waiter and looked back.

A man aged around forty was sitting behind him.

"Wait a minute, police are there in *mufti*", he whispered again without looking back.

Rahul got frightened with a chill going down his spine.

He slowly looked around to see whether anyone watching him. He felt nothing suspicious as none was looking at him.

Rahul wiped the sweat on his forehead and ordered for one more tea as he has to wait some more time sitting there.

'Are police really watching me?...everything has gone well from the morning....it would be good if this could be done smoothly', Rahul thought sipping the tea and looking around.

As he is taking tea for the second time after having puffed off three cigarettes, he could not feel the tea tasty.

Suddenly, the person came forward and sat down in front of Rahul.

Rahul looked at him anxiously.

"They have left", the man smiled looking straight into Rahul's eyes.

Rahul sighed in relief.

"You should keep an eye on police....we must be able to recognize police when they are in plain clothes", he seemed delighted in warning Rahul.

Rahul is anxious to complete the transaction and disappear from the place as quickly as possible.

He put his hand in his pocket and threw the last packet in front of the feet of the person.

The person looked down and nodded his head as if he observed it.

Rahul immediately got up and came out of the restaurant.

He swiped off the sweat again.

He felt relieved on finishing the task smoothly.

He looked in his mobile.

It is already 8.30 PM.

He took out the slip and searched for the payment procedure again.

He has to wait at Omega hotel again for receiving his payment at around 9.30 PM.

He called an Auto.

****

Rahul quickly ate two egg puffs and finished a cup of tea in Omega hotel. He could not get proper meal since the morning.

The hotel is still abuzz with night rush even at 10.30 PM. He came out of the hotel and lit a cigarette. He looked around to find whether someone is waiting for him.

'Spent much on Auto fares and cigarettes' he felt irritated over the tedious shuttling journeys he had to made since the morning.

"Did a good job...you got your payment", someone whispered from behind.

Rahul looked back.

A short Black young man is smiling.

He is not Jack.

He gestured Rahul with his eyes to look down on the floor. Rahul looked down and saw a paper cover in front of his feet. He bent down and picked up the cover. He felt something like folded currency notes in the cover.

Rahul looked around for the young Black.

He has already disappeared from there.

Rahul immediately put the cover in his pocket and started to walk towards his room as it is nearer to this hotel.

'Yes!', it is not a small thing!' he told himself lying down across the bed after completion of the recollecting process.

'I should ask for more transactions per day, so that the shuttling expenses could be managed', he thought.

He got the satisfaction that somehow he was able to get a job that is fetching good earnings.

He closed his eyes and fell into deep sleep as he was tired of the shuttling throughout the day.

****

CHAPTER EIGHT

Rahul woke up with the sound of continuously ringing mobile. He was in deep sleep and could have been got up only after a few more hours because of the tiredness of yesterday's assignment. He got up and sat down on the bed. He looked at his phone.

It is Jack!

He has come into his senses and looked for time.

It is already 15 minutes past 8 AM.

He lifted the call with a slight excitement to know why Jack is calling so early.

"Hello...Number Four! Hope you are happy with yesterday's earnings!", Jack's voice is enquiring.

"Yes... it was good!", Rahul replied with the satisfaction in his voice and also for calling him by some code number which gave him a sense of elevation.

"Good... you did the job smoothly... you have impressed us with neat handling of the transactions. Well... you should be careful with their presence or movements .... You should be very careful... They are everywhere .... At any cost... you should not be caught... okay?" Jack's voice turned commanding.

Rahul understood that Jack is very careful in mentioning the Police as *they*.

"I would be careful...yes...I will be careful about their presence", Rahul replied like a loyal worker because, the payment and appreciation made him feel to respond positively.

The amount he got after attending a risky as well as an exciting job he had attended made him elevated.

"Good... you would get a call on the morning if an assignment is there for that day.... You would have work load at least for fifteen to twenty days in a month... you know?....that means... enough rest for you as well...isn't it?....by the way...today you will receive a call for fresh assignment...number of transactions will be more...Best of luck!", Jack's call went off as if he is not ready for any further conversation with Rahul.

'Fine!.... that's good!...transactions will be more from today!... so I'll be able to cover my expenses and can be left with good margin too!', Rahul felt relieved with the confirmation received from Jack.

He kept his phone in his pocket and lit a cigarette.

He started thinking of what precautions he should take for smoothly finishing his daily assignments and safely escaping from the watching eyes of Police and CC cameras.

'I should be smart enough and more cautious to outwit the police surveillance while collecting and delivering the stuff', he thought.

His mobile started ringing again disturbing his thought process. He is startled over the sudden ringing sound of his mobile. He thought that Jack must be calling again. He took out the phone from his pocket.

It is from Imran!

He felt embarrassed to attend the call.

But he decided to lift the call as he is receiving a call from Imran first time after his departure to Mumbai.

"Hello...Imran!", Rahul lifted the phone.

He didn't feel interested to receive the call at this time.

"Hello Rahul! ..... How are you *Yaar*!? ... Seems you are very busy ... I called three times ... you didn't lift... what's the matter? ... got any job?.... or still searching?", Imran is in enquiry mode over his current position.

Rahul knows that wherever Imran would be, he always keeps thinking about him or rather worrying whenever Rahul loses a job and struggling to find a new one.

"Yes, I got a job", Rahul replied.

Rahul wanted to maintain it cool. He has decided not to reveal what is his new job.

"Oh God!... good news *Yaar*! ... Congrats!...I know you can manage anything!... what is that? ... salary will be okay?", Imran's voice filled with the happiness that his friend is out of problems.

"It is just like courier job .... Salary is good', Rahul is careful in his replies.

'Oh that sounds great... now you're a courier boy!...that sounds funny you know?....okay *Yaar*.... I will talk leisurely sometime later... seems you are tired and still sleepy... I am also going for duty...take rest...Okay!', Imran's call went off.

Rahul felt relieved that Imran had not prolonged the call.

His mind again fell back on to the job to be attended today as the work load would be more. As he felt thirsty after getting up and talking to two persons in different versions, Rahul stood up and got some water from the bottle kept on the kitchen platform. He came back and sat down on the bed.

He again started thinking of his daily routine with the new job. Since Jack has told him that he should be careful in handling the stuff without falling under the surveillance of police and CC cameras, he wanted to think over the action plan. He thought of his appearance and movements.

'I should buy a couple of caps and sun glasses and should use them alternatively from place to place ... so that recognising me would be difficult for them. I should also change my attire. It should be very simple... none should get attracted to have a glance at me.....Yes, it should be so normal.....I should keep some biscuit packets and a water bottle in a sling bag to take at intervals so that I can avoid spending time and money for outside food or snacks.....Wherever I go, my first priority should be to ensure whether there are any CC cameras fitted somewhere in that area..... Or whether any police presence or police vehicle movement is there... Yes... I should ensure that!....What should else be done?', Rahul felt satisfied with the way he is thinking on the precautions to be taken in performing his duty.

He came out of his thoughts as he heard door knocking sound. He stood up and opened the door.

Sheela is standing there with a broad smile.

Rahul felt uneasy with her presence at the moment as he was fully focused on something more important.

'Why she is coming so often?', he muttered under his breath.

She is sizzling in a rose colour dress.

The dress, fragrance, slight make up, the loosely knotted hair, matching nail polish... and the small rosy ear studs.....everything is indicative of the special care she has taken for her appearance for standing before him.

She is directly looking at him with fully widened and searching big eyes that are just killing with rapid movements.

Rahul is unable to look into her eyes. Even the quick glances thrown at her are causing his heart thumping with a fast beat.

"Hi Rahul.... Seems I disturbed your sleep. Yesterday you were late I think. Have you got a job?", Her concern is very much expressive in her eyes.

He is surprised over her focus on him.

'She must be watching my movements', He thought.

"I got a job... it is sort of courier job... salary is also good", Rahul simply repeated his replies to Imran expecting the same questions from her also.

"Thank God! ... Very happy to hear the good news in the morning itself! ... I should have brought some sweet! .... Anyway, congratulations Rahul!", her lips became thinner without losing the curve in the middle as she is smiling. Whenever, she is calling him by name, his heart is thumping with increased beat.

"Thanks!", Rahul replied with increased uneasiness as he never faced such a close interaction and chitchatting with any girl.

She looked at him with a broad smile and with a surprise element in her eyes just to indicate that he could know how to respond to a compliment.

Every time her presence at his room is nothing but dragging him into embarrassment. But somehow he is able to interact with her even by giving curt replies to the flood of queries coming from her.

He does not know whether he likes it or not. Now he is more embarrassed with her looks and felt puzzled why she is still standing in front of him even after informing her about his job position.

"By the way.... I came here now to tell you something.... I got an assignment sort of research assistant.... It's a government assignment... But it's an outstation project at New Delhi.... So I should be out of station for three weeks....tomorrow morning... I will be leaving for New

Delhi... Will you please drop me at airport in the morning!?', Sheela told the matter at a stretch as she knows pretty well that he doesn't show much interest on such interactions.

She looked at him expecting a simple positive response. Her eyes are expecting some congratulatory words from him on having got a government assignment too.

'Tomorrow morning I will also be out of station... urgent consignments should be delivered. Actually, I am leaving today itself', Rahul lied without looking at her.

He was surprised himself how he could lie so promptly and convincingly.

Sheela looked disappointingly. Rahul could see what her feeling is by making a simple glance at her.

She stood there motionless for a few seconds.

She had planned and visualized spending a lengthy session in his presence.

Actually her flight would start at 2.30 PM tomorrow. She has already made plans even for a lunch with him on the way to airport.

As he smashed all her little sweet dreams with his blunt rejection, it took her some time to respond.

"Oh...then it is okay... no problem...I will call my friend...she will accompany me to airport...okay Rahul... all the best!", she uttered the words in low voice.

She turned back and went down quickly much to his relief. Rahul waited till she disappeared from his sight. He closed the door and lit a cigarette.

'Girls always look for bodyguards for their safety and personal assistants for attending all their requirements...She is no exception... It is good that I was able to escape.... I should not give much scope to her to make frequent visits to my room... any further moving with her will not be good for my job.... now she will be out of station for three weeks.. It is okay for now... after that what?', he is thinking how to avoid her presence.

Suddenly, something flashed in his mind.

'Why should I be holed up here? .... Better to vacate this room and search for accommodation somewhere else ... away from this locality...so that I can avoid her and it would be safe for my movements too,' He came to a conclusion.

He looked around the room.

He has been residing here for the last four years.

'So far so good with this room .... Except the rent hike', He thought.

It's been comfortable for him to be secluded among the fully packed flats in the building.

'Now it is the time to move out', Rahul confirmed himself moving into bathroom.

****

CHAPTER NINE

Rahul woke up with the alarm tune of his new smart phone.

It is 6.00 AM.

He got up slowly from the newly bought bed though he disliked of leaving from it so early.

The Queen sized bed with eight inches foam mattress with matching pillows, two chairs, a dressing table set, the air conditioner filled the bedroom to make it comfortable in his eyes.

Wardrobe is filled with the branded clothes both casual and formal.

The bathroom is equipped with a geyser and costly range of toiletries.

An electric stove, frying pans, two small pressure cookers, other dishes, cutlery items and all the kitchen equipment required for cooking whenever he wants to eat at home covered the kitchen.

A double cushion sofa set, glass top coffee table, a wall fitted forty two inches sleek LED television set made the front room attractive.

Of all, the brand new laptop is the most loveable thing in his possession. Whenever he opens it, he feels like a software professional.

Though he prefers to live alone, he wanted to have all the comforts he can afford with his increased earnings.

Nowadays, as soon as getting up from the bed, it is a new habit for him to look around the flat that gives him a sense of satisfaction as if he has been elevated to a higher standard of living.

He brushed his teeth and got ready a cup of black coffee for stimulating his bowels.

He stood in the balcony of his new flat with the coffee cup.

'It's been almost three months since shifted to this flat', Rahul thought sipping the coffee.

Taking black coffee in the morning is a new habit he developed after coming to the new flat because he has to start for the duty early in the morning so that he could cover all the delivery points.

The balcony gives a panoramic view of the morning with the sprawling green turf like agriculture fields meeting the clear blue sky on one side, spreading skyscrapers vying among themselves on the other side.

He is in the top floor of a ten storied apartment block which is part of five such sky scrapers stood elegantly in a luxurious gated community provided with all the necessary amenities including a provisional store, swimming pool, spa, gym, children's play corner etc.

A lot of change has taken place in his life style within these three months after shifting to this well-furnished double bedroom flat in a posh locality which is far away from his old room.

In fact, it is located on the other side of the city at a distance of nearly fifty kilometers from his old room locality. The rent of the flat is five times what he was paying for his old junk room.

He felt lucky for he was able to shift to the new flat within four days after Sheela left for New Delhi. While vacating his old room, he told Sheela's mother that he was going to Mumbai as he got a job there.

'Now there's no contact link with old life around the old room', Rahul sighed in relief.

He has already deleted all the old contacts while replacing the old mobile with a sleek top brand smart phone.

Though he can afford to buy a two wheeler now, he didn't buy one because he prefers to travel in Auto which is more convenient and safe for his movements as part of his duties.

Now he is busy seven days a week. He is fully engaged in all activities of the drug supply chain. Number of stuff collections, transfers and deliveries increased.

He is meeting different persons involved in the field.

Daily, he has to meet those who bring the stuff to the city and those who distribute it according to the booking demand received through the network.

The entire system is working on a straight line hierarchy.

Jack is one of the top leadership of the trafficking syndicate which has been expanding its roots in the country for more than a decade. Jack acts as in-charge of all the activities related with drug trafficking in the city and other regions and districts of the nearby states. He plays a crucial role in selecting new recruits into the field. He monitors the activities of those from whom he chooses some probable bunch of persons and after confirming that they are safe for the field, he keeps studying their back ground and completes the final list once he is satisfied that they are the right choice for the field. He frequently goes out of country to place orders and to covert the money earned here into dollars.

Only as and when the money conversion is completed, shipment of new consignment is taken up.

The drug stuff enters the country either through western or eastern coastline. Once entered, it gets divided into parts and allotted to different cities.

The transportation to a city is generally done through trucks and containers where the drug packages are smartly hidden in the loaded consignments. As soon as the vehicle reaches the destination city, it stops at an assigned place where the packages are taken away by a core member.

The core members are most reliable ones.

The top leadership of the hierarchy takes utmost care in appointing the core members. It takes several years for a person to grow as a core member. Reliability and success rate in the tasks accomplished are the criteria based on which one grows in the field.

Rahul is set to become a core member soon.

Actually the top leadership picked up him to make him a part of the core team considering his background.

There may be just five or six core members working in a city circle who receive the stuff into the city and distribute the smaller consignments to vendors and through them to the delivery boys.

The vendors are very crucial because they act as the link between the demand and supply. As per the orders placed by them, the stuff enters into the city. They maintain the contact lists of the buyers who fall under two categories, either direct buyers or retailers.

The direct buyers belong to elite sections of the city. They are from all walks of life either private or government sectors.

The retailers are engaged for selling the smaller packages or packets to targeted sections which mainly comprises software employees and students who can't afford to buy directly.

The vendors get their commission as per the quantity ordered. Similarly, the delivery boys get the commission as per the quantity delivered.

It can't be certain that the stuff would come on a particular date. Arrivals depend on many factors.

The stuff is hidden in containers which are received from ports. Sometimes, the stuff reaches the coastline through small boats where it is handed over to the local vendors who in turn hide the stuff in the container laden trucks bound for the city. The entry of the container depends on delivery at port, loading into truck, arrival of truck into the city and at the spot where the stuff can be taken away from the container.

All the tasks are to be taken up as per the monitored instructions from the top hierarchy.

'How big the field is?', Rahul wondered finishing the coffee.

Apart from delivering the stuff, Rahul is now busy in contacting the buyers and attending stuff unloading duties also.

Today he has to look for the stuff arrival into the city.

Though he is a delivery boy for the sake of hierarchy, Rahul wonders how fast he rose in the field and how reliably he is being engaged with all the important tasks.

The top leadership did not believe him so easily.

Rahul really worked very hard during these three months. Actually, there has been a lot of transformation in his way of life and attitude and way of looking at an issue.

When occasions demanded, he had delivered the stuff for the entire city and adjacent towns also within twenty four hours not only once; he could do this exercise four times.

Two times when a vendor was not able to attend the orders from the buyers, he contacted them, collected the money and delivered the stuff smoothly.

Once, when he was assigned the job of unloading the stuff from a truck, he had to wait in the city outskirts for a whole day because the truck was stuck up in a traffic jam due to a serious accident on the highway.

Rahul reached the spot and spoke to the driver.

It was a fruits transporting truck.

The stuff was packed in wooden cartons and hidden below the fruits packed wooden cartons staked in top rows. But, because of continuous presence of traffic police and the highway being congested with hundreds of vehicles, he could not take out the stuff.

Rahul arranged a small van which was kept waiting in a nearby service road. He made several attempts to unload the stuff.

But, he could not succeed as there was no scope to unload the top rows of the cartons from the truck.

After waiting there over the night, the driver, by the dawn, was able to turn the truck into a service road where Rahul shifted the stuff cartons into a small van.

Of all, one incident made him the most reliable member in the eyes of the top hierarchy.

Just ten days ago, Rahul escaped from the trap of police so easily sensing their presence.

That day morning Rahul himself got the stuff unloaded from the truck and took away the three big size bags weighing around fifty kilograms to a flat which is treated as stock point.

A key of the house was given to Rahul for dumping the stuff.

He relies on small size goods carrier vehicles to take the bags to the stock point.

That is a rented double bed room in a busy residential locality and being used for more than five years.

The watchman of the building knows Rahul. As per his understanding the flat is being used as stock point for parcel or bagged consignments of a courier company.

Rahul has made friendship with him by making tips whenever he visits that place telling him that the bags contain chemical powder which is used as raw material for making medicines and cosmetics.

Half of the quantity received comes in small sachets and the bulk portion comes in medium size polythene packets with an outside paper cover. The packets are for retailers and some big or elite direct buyers.

Generally, direct buyers get the stuff in sachets received from the delivery boys. This stuff is enough for meeting the orders of a week.

He distributed the packets and sachets required for the day to the vendors so as to hand over to the delivery boys. Once that process was finished, he left the stock point and started to the selected meeting point where he was to handover the sachets to two persons who are direct buyers.

Rahul was waiting at a Pan Shop adjacent to a bus stop.

It was 4.30 PM.

The roads were slowly getting filled with the evening rush.

Rahul bought a cigarette in the Pan Shop and kept waiting for the first person.

The first person came ten minutes later than the time told him. He is a forty years old bald head person working in a private firm.

Rahul knew him because he met him six or seven times to handover the stuff. That man sells the sachets to software employees. He comes for the stuff at least once in three days. Recently, he increased the orders too. Whenever met, he flashes a broad smile as a token of wishing him.

Rahul is irritated that he was late.

As soon as seeing him, Rahul stepped forward and moved to take out the stuff from the sling bag.

Suddenly, he stopped and saw again into the eyes of that man.

Within five feet distance, Rahul could notice that he was not flashing any smile. His face was seen worried. His eyes are trying to tell that something was wrong. He was not moving forward. Once, Rahul stopped, he stepped back and was looking in some other direction.

Rahul sensed danger. He turned casually towards the Pan shop and lit one more cigarette and stood there as if he was waiting for his city bus.

That bald man took out his mobile from shirt pocket and started to browse as if he was also waiting for his bus.

While Rahul was trying to make a casual look on the surroundings just to find out whether there was anything dangerous which made the bald man worried, suddenly, two persons approached the bald man.

They were seen asking him for a while and a minute later, they took away him from the bus stop to a side lane. Rahul realized that they were cops in plain clothes. He felt a sudden jerk in his spine and his mouth got dried. He threw away the cigarette and slowly crossed the road and stood behind a group of customers who were standing and taking tea in front of a café. The café was just opposite to the lane into which the bald man was taken.

Rahul anxiously looked towards the lane where he saw that the four cops including the two who took him there were searching the bald man's pockets. His shirt was removed and pant fly was open. As they could find nothing, they patted his shoulder and let him go. Bald man was seen asking the Police with an innocent and surprise filled face, what was wrong with him and what they were searching for. Police didn't tell him and left from there after looking with probing eyes all over the area for some time. The bald man slowly came back to the bus stop and casually looked around for Rahul. As he could not find him, he left from there with a worried face.

But, Rahul waited there for some more time because the Police were standing nearer the lane and watching the people.

Suddenly, two of them crossed the road and started to probe in the crowd nearer to him. Rahul suppressed an urge to run from the place as any small suspicious movement was just enough to throw him into the risk of being spotted.

Rahul slowly went into the café and occupied a chair.

The café is full of evening crowd. While ordering for a cup of tea, he slid down his sling bag under the chair. On sipping tea for a while, he slowly stood up and came out. The plain clothed cops were still waiting there with probing eyes.

After watching the surrounding area for nearly twenty minutes, they left from there on bikes.

Till then, Rahul was sweating profusely. His shirt was drenched with heavy sweating under arm pits and back. He kept on wiping his face with hand kerchief.

After staying there for more than fifteen minutes, Rahul went back to his chair and took his bag and came out. He got into a city bus and left from there heaving a sigh of relief.

Later, he got a call from Jack.

Rahul told him what had happened. Jack's voice sounded worried. He asked whether they saw him. Rahul confirmed him that they had not seen him as he was able to cross the road and hidden behind some persons standing there. Jack strongly warned him to be more careful in future as more Police parties are on a hunting spree for drug traffickers all over the city.

Because of this incident, Rahul could not deliver the two consignments on that day. The bald man was asked to go underground for some time and Rahul has been assigned to deliver the stuff to some customers directly for the next ten days. After wards, a new person was engaged to look after the demand for that circle.

Since then, Rahul turned more cautious at all the assigned places and developed a habit of keenly observing and searching for plain clothed cops. Wherever, he felt suspicious, he keeps the stuff receivers get alerted with a pre-informed caution signal through his movements. Till he gives a green signal, the receivers should not approach him. With this new method, he has been able to pass on the stuff to the receivers smoothly.

Rahul felt proud that he is able to be smart enough in fooling the search parties. A couple of times, he suspected their presence and succeeded in identifying the plain clothed cops who were in search of drug traffickers. He has slowly improved his counter surveillance against the cops by keenly studying their movements. No sooner he has become an expert in spotting them by seeing their looks, attire and vehicles. Now he is also able to find even split teams based on their exchanged signals. Wherever he goes, his first focus point is locating the CCTV cameras of the area and how to escape from their coverage.

Once felt that he is in a safe position in all respects, he quickly delivers the stuff and vanishes from the scene within no time. With such a speed and technique, he has exceeded the set targets and improved the demand from new quarters too. The all-round success rate made him one of the most reliable members of the drug trafficking business in the city.

He has already got enough hints for his likely elevation as a top core member. Rahul wondered how much change has taken place in his life.

Suddenly, he got an urge to look at his image in the mirror. He stood before the dressing mirror in the bedroom. He saw at the trimmed beard. It looks like an add-on attraction to the cheeks that appear swelled slightly with an increased fat layer around his face. The hair style is looking good.

'They did a nice job!', he felt.

Now he is regularly going to the Men's Deluxe Saloon located in the gated community itself. They do all that what one needs to look good. His eyes are now wide and reflecting some unknown smartness hidden behind them. He kept watching his face for a while.

'Not bad....Yes...there's something new in my looks! That's nothing but the smartness! Without this smartness, it'd be very difficult to survive in this cruel world....Particularly, while working in this field....Yes...I'm smart enough to deal with every bloody idiot....my smartness has changed my life!...This hidden talent that had been dormant all these years has woken up and is giving good results!', Rahul gently patted his head while going to bathroom.

****

CHAPTER TEN

'What a heartless rugged idiot he is!?', Sheela cursed Rahul as a morning routine.

She is standing in her balcony.

It is already more than six months after she returned from New Delhi. All her efforts on finding his whereabouts were in vain. He left without leaving his traces. Though her mother told her that he left for Mumbai, she could not believe that. She strongly felt that he could not leave the city. She's felt ashamed of herself that she failed to trace him even having so much knowledge gained from her education and training.

As soon as getting up from bed, she comes out and stands in the balcony. It is the place where she likes to think about him.

Whenever she feels swarmed with his thoughts, she goes up to the terrace of the building and stands in front of his room as if he is there inside the room. But as days passed on, she stopped going up. Because, the lonely sight of the room standing at the corner of the terrace is so terrible to see....just like a haunted house shown in movies.

Though the owner of the building hanged a to-let board in front of the building, surprisingly, the room is still vacant for the last six months.

She got a dream last night. She tried to recollect it.

'It was really a peculiar visualization of wonderful imagination!', She thought.

The dream starts in Mumbai. How come she is in Mumbai?....Because, Sheela seems.... staying in Mumbai on some work. Perhaps... may be on duty. She is going by car...There she spots Rahul walking on footpath. She feels shocked seeing him there. He appears in a more pathetic condition than what she has last seen him in his room.... with worn out attire.....grown beard..... thinned down cheeks.... and with the same curled hair as if he just now got up from the bed. Sheela follows him without his knowledge. He stops at a road corner, approaches the crowd and starts begging them for his food. Sheela gets angry. She rushes towards him and pulls his shirt. Rahul looks back. He gets surprised seeing her in Mumbai. She chides and yells at him what he is doing here. She demands why he left without telling her. Rahul bows down his head just like what he used to do in their meetings at his old room. Then she holds his hand and drags him towards her. He comes so closed to her. She looks into his eyes and tells that now she is there to look after him. He starts crying. She hugs him and starts consoling him just like a kid. There ends the dream.

'How wonderful it would be, if it could happen that way!?', Sheela sighed with the relief resulted from memorizing the dream.

She had returned from New Delhi after staying there for more than two months and on completion of the multiple training courses successfully. The training helped her a lot by fetching her an assured career in a new field. But, she felt disappointed as Rahul left without leaving his traces. She planned to have an exclusive treat with him.

She cursed herself too for she ignored a compelling desire of asking him for his mobile number while she was leaving for New Delhi.

Initially, she felt like a child who is crying for a missing pet. She even chided her mother for letting him go without telling his future whereabouts in Mumbai.

Her mother suspected that something was there. She even asked her as to why Sheela was focusing more attention on Rahul. Sheela managed to curtail the conversation as if there is nothing more than just neighborhood necessities.

The emptiness that resulted on losing a valuable thing and vacillating thoughts around his memories made her mind disturbed a lot.

But, slowly she tried to make it a habit of falling into his memories only in the mornings and getting busy with the new job she got after her arrival.

She is now frequently visiting various places as part of her job. Three days ago, she returned from Ahmedabad after attending a small crash course related with her job.

This job has brought a sea change in her life. It is giving immense satisfaction apart from considerable earnings.

She is now experiencing new environment, meeting new persons, facing new situations, and learning new things. Moreover, new friends!

Particularly, she got a new friend Vineeta. She is expert in the application of informatics. She is teamed up with Sheela. With her help, Sheela could be able to solve many case studies duly applying the informatics in processing and analyzing various situations as part of her job. Sheela calls her 'Winnie' whenever she is in the teasing mood. Vineeta corrects it as 'Vinee'. Vineeta came so close to her just in two months as they have been involved in working together on almost daily basis. Actually Vineeta is surprised over Sheela's command on the subjects she is dealing with.

She wonders how she could find a quick solution for any problem.

Sheela is very happy to find a companion like Vineeta.

Every day, while proceeding with her job, is providing her a new scope for studying and finding something fruitful. It's challenging too. Life has become so busy. She felt it.

Her mother too noticed it. She has been watching Sheela becoming a busy person after stepping into this job.

'But she deserves it!', She feels.

She knew that since childhood Sheela is something special and different from other kids of her age group among her relatives or friends. She stood first in all classes since childhood. Though she was active and played games, she used to prefer to play and enjoy rather than winning the games. She prefers to watch and observe things around her. She never goes into arguments. She is a book worm. Her mother feels proud in telling others about her daughter.

'That's why she got this career', she feels.

She is happy that Sheela has got a career which she could get with her educational background. Moreover, she felt it a safe one as it is a government job.

Now her father is also happy that she has become an earning member which makes it easier for searching suitable matches for her marriage.

Her mother has already given enough hints to Sheela that they are already in search of suitable matches. Sheela gets angry and starts yelling at her mother to stop the topic right there as she is not interested in getting married so early.

Her mother reminds her that she has already twenty four years old and at her age she had been sending Sheela to school. Whenever, the topic of marriage comes, Sheela gets a feeling of missing something. That feeling turns into irritation which leaves her in a slight depression.

'He is the reason for all this nonsense!', Sheela frowns.

'When will you start for New Delhi again?....Tomorrow evening...right?', her mother asked her placing a cup of coffee in her hand.

Sheela has abruptly stopped her session with Rahul related thoughts and came into reality.

****

"Come quickly!. It is already late!....first you take charge of your consignment.....tell him to come ten minutes later. Quick!', Rahul cut the call.

He is waiting in the balcony of the stock point flat for the arrival of two core members as the stuff has already dumped there for distribution.

He is worrying that the core members are also not upto the mark set by the top hierarchy. Unless one sticks to time schedule, things do not seem moving smoothly and safely.

Rahul lit a cigarette.

Now he is a top core member! Most reliable member!

'Life has become so busy!', he thought.

He is in such a busy schedule that he is not able to spare enough time for proper sleep and even to eat something tastefully!

He is now playing many roles with his elevation as a core member. Jack burdened him to look all the activities of the city and got himself relieved because Jack wants to focus on neighbouring states and moreover, he is short of time to move out of the country for stuff bookings and money transfer work.

Though he has now become the top member after Jack, Rahul has never seen who are there in the top hierarchy.

Jack always refers to them as top bosses of the drug organization in the country. A couple of times, Rahul asked him who they are and where they stay. Jack laughed at him and told that it would be too risky to know about them.

'So it wouldn't be safe to see them!....why should I be so hurry to know about them as long as I am getting super earnings', Rahul shrugged to himself.

As being shouldered with the burden of the city, Rahul has become top boss of the city for all activities. All are turning to him for everything. He talks to other core members. He himself decides the quantity of the demand and places the orders for consignments. He engages members to unload the stuff arrivals.

He is now moving in four wheelers to roam in the city as his elevation into a core member put him into tight situation that forced him to get into new luxuries.

Sometimes he is having meetings in star hotels. He is spending lavishly on dining out and having working lunches or dinners with other members or sometime new parties or elite customers in the course of finding new demand.

He even engaged himself to find new recruits like him.

'How funny and tedious it would be in searching and finding guys like me!?' Rahul laughed inside recollecting his recruitment.

'Within six months, I have reached the top position in the city... Yes...it is something special!', he felt proud and turned back from the balcony to go inside as he spotted the arrival of the first core member.

The heroin powder packets and bags were stacked neatly in a bedroom. They were already got segregated as per area wise or party wise consignments. In all, there are two hundred small packets containing fifty sachets in each and thirteen bags containing big packets meant for bulk consumption.

'By tomorrow evening, the stock would be exhausted. Indent orders should be placed tonight', Rahul told himself.

He took the first consignment bundle which is to be issued to the core member who is coming up.

'How crazy this guys are to consume it? .... Idiots...don't know what to do with the money they have?.....what pleasure they would get in getting drowsed and lying down like a useless log?' Rahul wondered.

He doesn't like to consume it. He has never tasted it since touching the first sachet Jack had offered to him.

He doesn't like to be weak.

For that matter, he has never consumed liquor too in his life. He is fond of good food which he craved for when he was an orphaned child. His only companion for all occasions is smoking. He got this habit from Imran. Both started smoking cigarettes after strongly confirmed themselves that it was the only aide that acts as a stimulant of thoughts for improving their livelihood.

****

'What Salman! What are you doing? What about Suneel? You are just sleeping.....I told you all to be alert...keep a continuous watch on those buggers!...Don't tell me useless stories.. I want results...okay?', Inspector Vinay yelled over his mobile at one of his tipping aides.

Sub-Inspector Raghu is sitting in front of him and simply watching him.

They both just have returned from the ACP office where they had to face a strong dose of scolding from ACP as media exposed increased drug usage in the areas falling in their jurisdiction. Since last night TV channels have been repeating a video clipping of two youngsters smelling white powder on a paper sitting at a corner inside a pub. Though police raided the pub, they could not find anything. Two days ago, a news item appeared in two local newspapers that a teenager was found lying unconsciously on the premises of his school. His friends revealed that he consumed some drug.

The ACP shouted at Vinay and warned him to come back to him only after catching at least one drug trafficker. He was angry as he had already tasted the wrath of the Police Commissioner who had to face a volley of questions from the print and electronic media about the failure of the police in busting the drug usage in pubs.

After venting out his anger at the tipping aides, Vinay leaned back in his chair.

He never saw ACP in such a bad mood and moreover what irked him a bit more is that he never received such a direct scolding from him. He has been in the good looks of his boss so far.....dearer to him. He received a lot of appreciation from the top ranks. But, now he has to face rebuke too.

'We should engage more man power Sir!...Otherwise, it would be difficult to trace them', Raghu tried to change the ambience.

'Why are you telling all such useless trash sitting in front of me?,,,Why didn't you do that!?....I've already told you to engage Salman brothers too. But you couldn't do that...Now you are simply giving me wonderful advices!...and these fellows are roaming the city on personal and fetching works, I know everything! ', Vinay turned his anger towards Raghu and his team.

The three constables, who are standing behind Raghu, are silently looking sideways on confirming themselves that the boss is not in good mood.

'I will be on that job Sir, I will talk to him right now', Raghu got up from the chair and moved out sensing that it would not be safe to hang around there in that room. He knows that it would not be so easy to engage more manpower.

'The more men engaged... the more money to be paid. Where to get the money?', Raghu muttered himself while moving out of the station.

****

Rahul came out of bathroom after having enjoyed a good bath under shower.

Calling bell is ringing.

He went to the front room and opened the door. Zomato boy is waiting with food he ordered for.

Rahul looked at the wall clock.

It is already 3.15PM.

He took the parcel and closed the door. He is tired and hungry. After finishing the tedious work load since last night, he returned to his flat about an hour ago.

He opened the food parcel.

The mutton biryani is still steaming with spicy smell that immediately made his mouth choking with water.

He opened the other parcel too. He took out a piece of crunchy chicken steaks. As he didn't eat anything since last night, the food he likes has turned tastier.

He switched on the TV while keeping his mouth busy in enjoying the well-cooked mutton pieces getting melted down in the mouth itself. All the items are tasty and got an enhancement with his craving hunger.

Rahul looked at the TV as he heard a news item on drug trafficking. He stopped eating for a while. The news reader is saying that with the increased drug trafficking in the city, police are facing a lot of flak from all sides. An opposition leader appeared on the screen. He is making a broadside attack on the government with strong criticism that the situation is so alarming just because the top leaders from the ruling party are behind the drug mafia.

Rahul laughed to himself. The news is still continuing. Now it's the turn of City Police Commissioner. He is talking in front of the News Channels. He told that police found that drug consumption has increased three times in the last few months and police were striving very hard to find the roots of the drug trafficking set up and soon they were going to bust the gang behind it. He appealed the public particularly, youth not to get addicted to drugs as it spoils their lives.

'Go to dogs! Who cares you? They got the money and they are enjoying it!', Rahul laughed chewing the chicken steak.

He felt it funny to watch the news. Watching such news in TV has become so interesting for him. In fact, it is the main purpose for buying the TV set. It has become a habit for him to search and watch news items about drugs.

He switched off the TV as he finished his lunch. As he was so hungry, he could finish the entire parcel. He lit a cigarette with a satisfaction of cooling down the burning appetite with a sumptuous biryani.

'Now the money collection and distribution have become big tasks!' Rahul felt.

Now he is looking after the money transactions with the help of two other core members. The accountal of the daily collections received from the consignees, and the daily payments made to those involved from the top to bottom that means, from the core members to delivery boys and others who stand as helpers in the field. All the records are being maintained at the stock point only. After he took charge, Rahul made the transactions very prompt and meticulous. All the money received in a day gets distributed on the same day or at the most, by the morning of next day. After clearing the payments, the remaining amount which stands around fifty to sixty percent, is credited in three bank accounts. That job is done by one senior core member. Rahul doesn't know whose accounts are these. His job is just to handover the remaining amount in three bags to the core member.

'Why should I bother about that?', Rahul avoided thinking too much about the money transactions as he is getting enough earnings.

After his elevation, his earnings are rising up. With the rise in the quantity brought into the city and the increase in the demand for the stuff, his share has also kept rising.

'I've never dreamt of such income!', Rahul wondered. Now it is becoming a head ache for him what to do with the rising income. He is spending lavishly. Now he is moving in cabs. Eating out in best restaurants and hotels. Living in a luxurious flat in a posh locality. Buying whatever home appliances and accessories he likes in the market. He is regularly shopping for new clothes. Now he is going for top brands. After spending a lot, still he is left with lot of money. He doesn't know what else he can do. He opened a savings bank account and started to transfer some money into it. He prefers to keep the remaining amount in the flat. He felt it would be risky if the entire money is credited into his account.

'What to do with the money?', Rahul thought for a while.

He wanted to count how much money he kept in the flat. He went into the bed room. He searched for and found the key of the cupboard which he hides behind the shaving kit in the bathroom. He opened the cub board. The money is kept in a medium size plastic box in the last rack behind some old clothes.

He counted the money. It is around three lakh and fifty three thousand rupees. The amount he saved in his bank account is about one lakh and ten thousand rupees.

'Wow! Good amount!', Rahul felt happy and while keeping the box back in its place carefully.

****

CHAPTER ELEVEN

Rahul woke up with continuous ringing of his mobile. It's seven in the morning. Last night he went to bed late as he was engaged in talking late night about the new stock arrivals in the city. He got up from the bed and looked at his mobile.

It is Imran.

Imran called several times within these six months. But Rahul could not lift his calls many times. He hardly talked to Imran that too for not more than four times. The situations compelled him to ignore the calls from Imran.

Today he is in good moods. He lifted the call.

"Imran! How are you?", Rahul's voice turned soft.

He is the only friend he could earn in his life.

"Hello *Yaar*!..My God!...today you have lifted the call....thanks for that...I am fine Yaar! seems you are so busy these days after joining this job!...Any way.....how is life?...hope you're doing well....today I made this call to share with you an important and good news!", Imran is unstoppable.

Seems, he is also in good moods.

"Yes Imran, because of these shift duties you know!...the job is like that, I could not respond...I am also fine... yes, life's become so busy....what's the matter!?' Rahul wanted to know that what made Imran so happy.

"The good news is .....My wedding's fixed!....I am going to marry!", Imran exclaimed.

Rahul could clearly hear the boyish shyness mixed with youthful joy in his voice.

"Congrats!...that's really a very good news!...I am very happy to know that.....who's that fortunate girl!....where from!.....there at Mumbai?", Rahul felt the real happiness in sharing the news.

It is a surprise for him to share such things. His reciprocation is also new to himself. He could not believe that he could speak so positively in such occasions.

"Thank you *Yaar*!....Thanks for the wishes....whom else...Rahul!....I can share such good news with you only!", Imran's voice turned emotional.

Rahul could hear the choking voice over phone.

"Okay..Imarn...that's okay...how is the girl...you liked?...She must be beautiful...otherwise you don't accept normal looking girls...Isn't it..? Didn't you tell me that?", Rahul voice turned into teasing mood.

"Oh my God!...Rahul you are talking like a new person!....my God!...I can't believe this!...Okay fine *Yaar*....yes it's your turn...Okay tease me....what's there?...I feel happy to listen such words from you...Isn't it?....How can I tell about the girl?...You should tell that....I'm sending her photo in Whatsapp...see yourself", Imran is really unstoppable with elated joy.

Rahul checked in his mobile and opened the post sent by Imran. Two photographs of a girl aged around twenty were sent. One is in sitting posture in a maroon color dress...sitting on a chair below a tree perhaps, at her residence and she is standing in the same place in a colorful saree in the other photo.

'Yes!...She is beautiful...looking like a lower middle class girl....seems well suitable to him', Rahul felt satisfied himself keenly looking the photos. 'Her eyes are big and attractive....Her smile too very nice', Rahul told himself silently looking at the posts.

"Rahul!....Hello....are you there?...Have you seen the photos?...How is she?", Imran's voice clearly reflecting the excitement for knowing the approval from his close friend.

"Beautiful Imran!...really she looks very good!...nice match...perfectly suitable for you...Congrats!", Rahul responded whole heartedly.

"Oh my God!....Thank you *Yaar*!...Thank you very much...I was worrying how you'd react!...You said Okay...But...this is true....you're talking differently...Yes...By the way...she is from our city... living there....actually, this match was brought by Mastan....you know...even I left him and came here...he helped me...must be thankful to him", Imran is still unstoppable.

"Oh!...that girl belongs to our city!...well.....that's really good to hear...Okay...Congrats again!", Rahul felt happy that Imran is still connected to this place.

"Thanks *Yaar*!...I'm happy today you're talking a lot and spending more and more time talking to me...that's giving me more pleasure...by the way, the girl's family is just ordinary one...Her name is Nazriya!...But...She looks like Shradda Kapoor....Isn't it?....She lost her father three years ago....Her elder sister already got married....She is living with her mother...Studied upto School final....She is twenty one years old....you know I'm twenty five now...She is five three...My height is five nine...right match you know....Last evening I spoke to her...you know...in Whatsapp video call....Of course...in her mother's presence only......She asked me about my job....She directly told me that she liked me *Yaar*....Her mother also talked very well ....And you know the real funny thing?....Nazriya is a Ladies Tailer!", Imran concluded with a big laugh.

"Oh!....That's wonderful!...Good...Made for each Other!...In all respects!...Congrats for that too!....Then....When?", Rahul felt this lengthy conversation with Imran is really very soothing to his mind.

It is just like the process of filling up an unwanted vacuum with cool water.

"Nikah will be held on Twenty eighth of next month Yaar!...That means one and half months from now...In the mean while...I'm coming there by the end of this month and I'll introduce you to them...We will go there... Be ready...please don't tell that you won't have time...Right?" Imran stopped to get the positive confirmation from him.

"Oh.....You're coming!....Come on!...Sure...I'll be there....We'll go and meet her!", Rahul confirmed.

He too got some excitement that he is getting involved in some social and family events which are very new to his life.

"Thank you very much Rahul!...I'm very happy today...I talked a lot and shared so much happiness with you...You know?....You and me...we're grown up as orphans....Now marriage is giving me a family...It's really a great and new feeling Yaar...Yes...We need family...What about you Rahul? You too need a family...By the way...How is Sheela...Any progress?", Imran wanted to hear some positive reply from Rahul.

"Why her topic now? I told you I'd left the place... Now I'm far away from that place...Don't know about her...She's not suitable for guys like me Imran...Leave it...It's about your marriage...Let's be happy about that...Right!", Rahul wanted to stop the unwanted irritation getting crept into the situation.

“Okay then...Take care...I’ll call later...Bye!”, Imran ended the call leaving him too satisfied.

Rahul opened the Whatsapp post sent by Imran. He looked at her photos again.

‘Really she is beautiful with a fair complexion...particularly her eyes.... They are big and lively... her smile gets reflected in her eyes’, he thought.

‘So...Imran is going to get into new life!’, he turned into brooding mood.

‘Really, Imran has got some meaning to his life! All the troubles....hardships...hunger...struggle for finding income to meet both ends...he has undergone a lot of bitter experience together with him!’, Slowly, Rahul started to recollect the first meeting with Imran.

Ten years ago, when he first entered the city, he was alone. He used to sleep on footpaths or bus stop shelters.

He tried to get a job for his survival. Soon he got a cleaning job in a restaurant. He felt happy that he could eat as much as he wanted. Though he worked hard throughout the day, nothing much could be left for him after the senior servers and cooks grabbed the entire left over food items. Twice he was thrashed by them for stealing the food hidden in the kitchen. He used to weep sitting alone in the backside of the kitchen.Many times, he had to live on eating the food left in the plates by the customers.

After struggling there for nearly more than a year, he left the job. Then he joined in a garage as assistant for mechanics. But, that was terrible. He had to work without leisure for at least half an hour. As he could not bear it for long, he quit it.

Then he was again in search of jobs. He did many jobs. He could not recollect which job he did after which one he quit.

One day evening, after finishing his duty at the printing press, he came back to the abandoned building which he had been using as his sleeping shelter along with two others. It was used as office building to the adjacently located spinning mill and was abandoned as the mill was closed long ago. Rahul and two other guys were using the main hall of the building as sleeping area sharing a corner each for the last three months. Slowly, it started to rain. After a while it turned into heavy rain. Soon the road in front of the building was flooded with rain water flowing to the downwards of the area. Soon the road disappeared under a gushing water flow which resembled like a small canal. Rahul was alone. He was happy that he could bring his food packet along with him. The evening was already turned dark as power went off. There were no street lights in that area. He could see the flow only in the blinking lights from a faraway place. Perhaps the lighting was of a factory which was running on generators. The water flow was very fast because it was being drained into a big drainage, a few feet right side of the building. The drainage was flowing under a culvert across the road. Everything was silent except the sounds of the heavy rain, the flow and its confluence with the water overflowing in the drainage. The sky was overcast and the clouds were thundering and lightning.

Suddenly, in a flash of lightning, Rahul found that somebody was getting drifted away in the flow. It was moving towards the drainage flow. He immediately jumped into the flood water flow and moved towards the direction in which way the body was dragged by the flow. Though he groped in the darkness, his hands could not find anything. He stood up and tried to see around if anything appears.

Water was flowing upto his waist. In a sudden flash of lightning, he could clearly see that it was a boy who was holding a small tree on the edge of the drainage and was trying hardly to escape from the force of the water flow. Rahul quickly moved and swam towards him. There he could see him because of the faint lighting coming from the faraway place. He tried to reach the tree. But water force was very strong. It was forcibly dragging everything into the drainage flow because of the low gradient. He forced himself towards the edge of the road where water flow was weak and from there he moved towards the tree. Now he came very close to the tree. He stood up and jumped towards the tree. As he could touch the lean trunk of the tree, he held it tightly and searched for the boy. He could see his head and hands which were holding the trunk in the opposite direction. The boy was getting floated in the water and would be forced to get dragged down into the swirling drainage flow at any movement. Rahul stood up and leaned towards the tree. Then he clung to the tree trunk with his legs and searched for the boy.

He got hold of a hand and yelled, “Hold my hand!”.

The boy loosened his grip around the trunk so as to get hold of Rahul’s hand with one hand. But, as his strength was not enough, he lost the grip and got drifted away towards the drainage. Rahul immediately jumped from the tree towards that direction and stretched his hands towards him. Luckily, he caught hold of a leg of the boy at the last movement as he was already being dragged head on into the gushing drainage flow. Though Rahul held his leg firmly, he was not able to hold it for long as he himself was getting forced towards the drainage flow. Rahul searched with his left hand in the water for support. He found a boulder at the edge of the drainage. He lied on it and forced his body onto it while pulling the leg of the boy towards him. Because of the support of the boulder, he could succeed. He completely pulled the boy towards him. On finding the support, the boy clung to Rahul's body with his hands and hugged him tightly. Though lying down on the boulder on his back, Rahul was unable to bear the force for long as the water force was heavy. Because of his force and the additional weight of the boy on his body, he was getting a lot of pain in his back. Now his hands were free. So, he searched for something in the water. He could touch a bigger boulder than what he leaned upon. Slowly, he moved towards the bigger one along with the boy who was clinging to him firmly like a baby monkey embracing her mother. With much effort, he could reach onto it. Now he could lie down on it along with the boy. The flood water is flowing upto his chest with dragging force. He looked around. He saw a small tree on his left side. By firmly pushing his feet on the boulder, he leaned towards his left side and stretched his hand towards the tree. After a few trials, he could catch hold of the trunk of the tree. On getting sufficient support from the grip of his hand around the tree, he dragged himself along with the boy towards the tree. Both of them could reach onto the ground level. Rahul slowly stood up with the support of the tree. Now the force of the flow reduced. The flood water was upto his thighs. Though the boy also stood up with his support, still he did not loosen his grip around him. Rahul waded through the water and brought him to his shelter. The boy crouched down in the corner where Rahul sleeps. Rahul removed his wet clothes and wrapped a towel around his waist. He was shivering and in shock. Rahul lit a candle with the match stick. The boy was around fifteen years old. He looked at Rahul with folded hands.

"Use this", Rahul threw his old nicker towards him.

He stood up and changed into the nicker and dried up his hair and body with the towel Rahul gave him.

"How it happened?", Rahul asked looking at him.

"I was going home....Suddenly rain started...I waited for half an hour in the backside lane. Then I tried to cross the road as flood water was rising on my side. But I slipped and fell down in the water which dragged me upto here...Thanks for the help!", the boy told with a gasping voice.

He was looking at Rahul. His eyes were reflecting the gratitude that he would have died in the drainage flow if this youngster had not saved him.

"Okay....you can't leave till the morning...better stay here tonight", Rahul told him.

He nodded his head in consent as he was not in a position to move from there because of the heavy downpour and the darkness.

It was around 9.00 PM. Rain slowly turning into drizzling. Rahul felt hungry. He opened the food parcel. There were three *Chapatis* and potato curry. Rahul offered the *Chapatis* to him. He took one *Chapati* and started to eat. Rahul finished his part quickly. The boy finished eating. After throwing away the parcel covers, he slept on the mat offered by Rahul.

By next morning, Rain completely stopped. Morning Sun was bright as if nothing happened. Rahul woke up. The boy was not there. It was around 7.30 AM.

'Must have gone home', Rahul thought.

But, the boy came back to him in the evening.

"Morning I had left silently as you were fast asleep", His voice was soft and apologetic.

"It's okay...no problem", Rahul replied as a matter of fact.

"You saved me...without you, I would have died in the drainage flood...Thank you very much", His voice was slow and very soothing to here.

"What's there? Anybody could do that?" Rahul shrugged.

"By the way, I am Imran... What's your name?", He asked stretching his hand forward for a hand shake.

"Rahul!, Rahul shook his hand as a formality.

"You offered me food last night. Now I've brought food for us. Let's eat!....It's *Chicken Biryani*!...You'd like it!", Imran exclaimed taking out a big food parcel from the plastic cover he brought.

Rahul suddenly felt hungry on hearing what he had brought. Both sat down for eating. It was a big parcel. The Biryani was steaming with nice smell of the spices.

"I'm working in a tailoring shop at Narayanapet area"....What are you doing?", Imran's voice reflected curiosity.

He seemed to know more about his life saviour.

"I'm working in a printing press", Rahul said while chewing the well-cooked leg piece.

He does not like to share much about him.

"That's a nice job *Yaar*!...I don't know what to do in printing press. All such jobs are different...All I know is tailoring. For the last three years, I have been working there...By the way...Why are you here?...Where are your parents?", Imran became an embarrassment for Rahul as he kept on creating hurdles while he was enjoying the Biryani.

"They were no more...I lost them in my childhood...I came here one and a half years ago from my village...since then I tried many jobs...presently this one...I'm staying here just for time being. Soon I'll shift to some working hostel or something like that", Rahul explained the position at a stretch so that Imran would not be left with any scope for further interrogation.

"Oh! you too an orphan!....I too lost my parents...My father died when I was a small kid...my mother died of illness when I was studying eighth standard...I had to stop education...My cousin joined me in this tailoring shop...Since then I've been working there. I'm taking shelter at the residence of one my distant relatives. It is nearer to the tailoring shop", Imran slowly explained his background as if he was telling an emotional story.

Suddenly, Rahul stopped to eat and looked at Imran. He got some intimate feeling about him.

'So....everywhere it is the same story!....Life of children who lost their parents must be miserable!', Rahul thought.

The biryani turned tastier now as he was eating together with a suitable companion for the first time.

Rahul came into the present with a touch of cool air. The fan is running in full speed. He saw around. He was sitting in the sofa in the drawing room of his flat. As his mind was lingering around his first meeting with Imran, he didn't observe when power went off. As the power is on, now the ceiling fan brought him back to the present tense.

He sighed with a satisfaction that Imran is getting a family soon.

'Then what about me?....Should I also get married and find a family?...Who will marry me?...As Imran said Sheela would marry me?...Should I ask her?...Am I suitable for her?', Rahul turned broody.

Suddenly, Sheela's face flashed in his mind. Her big eyes...they sparkle and move so quickly like a couple of swimming fish in tune with her expressions. Her lips...turn into different curves and stretches as per the length of her smile or speech.

Rahul lit a cigarette.

'Now I'm earning hugely....I can easily run a family...If I plan properly and strive a bit more hard,...soon I would be able to buy a house and a four wheeler too and provide all the needs for a family to live on comfortably....Then, I'm also eligible for marriage!...But Sheela fits into this?', he thought for a while on that.

'Who is Sheela?...She is a lower middle class girl...As she's been brought up by caring parents, she's grown up with a way of life suitable for her background...She is well educated...Naturally, she wants to have some decent life...She would certainly like to choose her husband who should also be well educated....Should be from a decent background...Should be doing a good job.....If the story goes like this....Can I fit into the frame?', He questioned himself while deeply puffing the cigarette.

'No...I'm not the right match for her. First of all, she doesn't accept me. She likes me because of that incident only. Any girl who is rescued from such a dire situation thinks so...Yes!...That's it!...No more foolish ideas about her...I should focus on my work first...It's changed my life', Rahul threw away the cigarette butt and opened his laptop to make some important entries about his daily transactions.

****

CHAPTER TWELVE

Inspector Vinay is sitting in his cabin and keenly watching the CCTV footage clippings on his desktop.

"These two are from Sunil Sir! ... See the third one...it's clear here! The packet is being exchanged...That bugger must be delivery man.. See Sir, he is handing over the packet to that school boy...rascal!," Sub-Inspector Raghu is furious while explaining each of the clipping.

They got the latest footages obtained from various spots which have been kept under surveillance.

"Yes ... it's a boy...this is a well-known public school...isn't it? ... corporate school.....run for elite sections...parents join their children paying huge fees...for the great facilities and quality education....and they are learning these things!", Vinay sighed.

'The boy is a teenager...he must be studying eleventh or twelfth standard...he is able to pay huge amount for buying drugs...damn it!...society's fast doomed to worst levels!', he fumed without knowing whom to blame on.

The boy was seen coming from the back side entrance of the school and stood at a corner of the compound wall. He waited there for a few minutes. A man, who was standing a few feet away from the boy, moved towards him pressing a mobile to his right ear as if he was talking to somebody. While crossing the boy, he casually handed over a cover to him. The boy quickly kept it in his bag and rushed into the school premises.

Vinay clicked the mouse for another clipping. He was surprised on seeing the same boy in that too.

"What!? .... the same boy again!? .... He's again seen with the same guy! ...what's the date?", he looked at Raghu with surprise filled eyes.

In this clipping also, the boy was seen receiving a packet from the same person. But this time, the place of exchange was a little farther than the earlier clipping. The process of exchange was the same. The man was seen talking to somebody over his mobile.

"That's of three days later Sir...that means, this mafia has already changed these children into drug addicts!...we have to check how many children got plunged into this hell....poor fellows!", this time it is Raghu's turn to fume.

"What are the other inputs from Sunil?", Vinay asked with a big sigh of relief and satisfaction.

"He is keeping an eye on that boy Sir...... every day a BMW drops and picks up him....must be rich...Sunil would come with full details tomorrow morning... he is on that job...already one more person has been engaged to track that delivery person too", Raghu is brimming with confidence because they have got some breakthrough in cracking the ongoing drug racket.

"We should bust this gang Raghu!...the situation is alarming...school level students and teenagers became addicts....we don't know how far it's already spread...really we should be ashamed of the situation...damn it!...we are sleeping all these days!', Vinay's voice sounded his anguish on failing to have proper control over drug trafficking in the city.

Certainly, he will have to face the wrath of ACP who in turn has to stand before the Commissioner of Police with an explanation.

"Tonight we'll get all the information Sir! ,,,,, then we can make a move with proper planning", Raghu played the consoling role to pacify his boss as well as to cover his failure too.

"Okay...let's see...try to get all the information", Vinay got up to leave for home.

His mind is disturbed with this incidence.

'Drugs even entered into school premises', he felt worried. Because this may spread to all educational institutes soon. His elder son is studying in one of such corporate schools.

****

"Hello!...number four....what's the matter?....Why at this time?" Jack's voice is hoarse as usual but sounded casual.

He responded to Rahul's call after several attempts.

"Have you seen the news in the TV?", Rahul came to the point.

On seeing the breaking news in the TV, he got frightened. All the channels are repeating a news item as breaking news. A person was caught by city police as he was supplying drugs to a student of a corporate school in the city. He searched all channels. The press meet is live and so being telecast as it is a sensational news for media.

"What news? What happened?", Jack became attentive.

"Just now Police Commissioner is telling in a press meet that they have caught a person while supplying stuff to students...that guy is not in our group...his face is covered....but I could recognize if he is in our group...he is tall...I'm sure none is so tall in our delivery boys... he doesn't belong to our set up...then who is he?...so far schools or students are not in our demand list...then who is this guy?...normally we don't' have demand coverage to that school area...actually the nearby areas are looked by someone whom I have appointed three months back.....but this is a different person...who is he?", Rahul's voice is tense as he is puzzled on watching this breaking news.

While he is talking to Jack, he got missed calls from two core members. They must be watching the news.

"Is it?...which area?...I'll check and come back to you", Jack's call went off.

Rahul is still sitting in front of TV in his flat. The breaking news is still being telecast as it is really a big thing for media. Even half an hour passed, he has not received a call from Jack. In the meanwhile, he responded to the calls of two core members who had called him while he was talking to Jack. They were worried and told that they didn't know that person. Rahul felt nervous. He lit a cigarette.

'Then who is this guy?....what would happen now?...that guy will tell everything about the drug field...then, everyone in the field would come into the frame....what should I do?...Jack must tell that!', Rahul is thinking.

As no call is coming forth from Jack even after an hour passed, Rahul felt restless. His mind is filled with some unknown fear that he never felt in his life. He made a call to Jack.

"I don't know that person", Jack responded.

His voice is tense now.

"Then who is he?...I didn't appoint him...none of our group never stands so foolishly in the coverage areas of CC cameras...I have just now confirmed from our core members too that they didn't know him... if he is not our man, then he must be working for others....but, as far as I know and as far as you put it that, ours is the only group which is involved in this!", Rahul stopped to take breath as his voice turned so tense and reflecting his fear.

He is eager to hear what Jack will tell.

"Let's us wait...stop making calls to me for a week...till next Monday...they must be on the tracking job...so let's be silent", Jack's call cut off.

Rahul is disappointed. He did not expect that Jack would respond in a callous way. He expected that Jack would react seriously and would engage him on the task of finding the details of the person who was caught so foolishly and where from he got the stuff.

Rahul lit a cigarette and went to his balcony.

'Why Jack was not serious about it?...why he was evading to act swiftly? first of all, who's this person?, How foolish were these transactions? with school going children!...really senseless!....whose idea is this?....why Jack wanted to be silent till next week?...What should I do now?....if Jack said so...arrival of the next consignment tomorrow would be doubtful!...police must have got all the information from that person...will they find us?....will they catch me?...what should I do now?', he felt a chilling shiver along his spine.

The thoughts about the incident are swirling in his mind just like the smoke emanating from the cigarette. He did so many jobs. But he never involved in unlawful activities in the past. Even after joining the field also he was careful about police vigilance. Many times, he could escape from surveillance teams and patrolling parties. Because, he was confident that he could manage his transactions out of their surveillance. But, for the first time, he felt that he is afraid of police because he is fully involved in drug trafficking.

'If they smell, they can trace me!', he shivered again.

Suddenly, the thought of stock point struck to his mind. The balance stock should be disposed by tomorrow morning. It would be risky to keep the stuff in the stock point.

'I should hand over it to the delivery boys as per the schedule....otherwise, police may trace the stock point too....the watchman knows about the transactions....perhaps, he doesn't know what is there in the bags!', Rahul's thoughts went on.

He opened his laptop and checked the list of scheduled deliveries. Fifteen sachets should be issued to a delivery boy and one big packet is to be handed over to a core member. Rahul made calls to both of them. The core member responded first. His voice was tense. He told that he was not in a position to come and collect because of the tightened police surveillance. The delivery boy lifted after several calls. He said that he was out of station because his mother was ill.

Rahul understood that he was lying.

He realized the situation.

'They won't take risk now....I should see that the stuff should be disposed at any cost....otherwise, I would be in risk', he thought for a while.

'I should myself get into the job....there's no option', he decided.

Suddenly, he thought of the payments due for him. From last week's collections, he made payments to all the delivery boys and one core member. An amount of around seventy thousand rupees is still pending with Jack. It is big amount. Next week the stuff arrival is doubtful as Jack wanted to be off for a week.

'Better I should get my money', Rahul thought.

He made a call to Jack. His phone is out of network. He tried several times but no use. Rahul realized that Jack has gone underground.

Slowly, sweating started to on his fore head. Suddenly, he felt alone.

'Okay...first of all, I should get rid of the stuff as soon as possible.....moreover, I can take the entire amount to be received from the parties so that payment due for me could be adjusted', he decided to get into the field himself.

Earlier also he delivered stuff to the customers after being elevated as a core member. He searched for the contact list in his laptop. The sachets delivery is a place located at a distance of fifteen kilometers from the stock point and the big packet has to be delivered five kilometers from the stock point but in the opposite direction. He decided to dispose the big packet first because it is nearer to the stock point. He got up to get ready for going to the stock point.

*****

"We have zeroed in on the area Sir, he must be residing there only", Sub-Inspector Raghu handed over a slip containing the details of the area in which the delivery man who handed over the drug packets to the boy at the school.

"What's the status now?", Vinay asked him while looking at the slip.

"We have engaged two constables along with one informer to follow his movements....still now, he is at home.....and about this boy...he is studying twelfth standard....his father is a businessman involved in spices exports...big business...close to some prominent political leaders too!", Raghu said handing the file containing the details of the boy to Inspector Vinay.

Vinay looked at the photos of the boy and his father. The boy looks innocent. His father is in his forties and his smile reflects the confidence that he can handle anything. He examined the details of the support and clout he is having in political circles. The details include two central ministers, one state minister and a few political leaders including the opposition leaders. Particularly, a relative of the state minister is so close to him and also is a sleeping partner in one of his business firms. Vinay wondered how politics and business have got merged into a confluence of mutual interests.

"So what shall we do about the identity of this boy? His father's highly influential....we should talk to ACP before making the press meet", Vinay looked at Raghu thoughtfully.

"Yes Sir, highly influential!...you need to talk to ACP Sir well in advance!", Raghu endorsed his view.

While he is getting ready to have lunch before meeting the ACP, his land line phone rang up. It is from the ACP. He took the receiver with beaming confidence in his face.

"Good afternoon Sir!,....yes Sir....thank you Sir...yes Sir...we're getting ready the file with all the details Sir...we'll come by three pm Sir...Sir, one thing...the family of the boy is highly influential...I'll explain the details in person Sir, thank you Sir...pardon Sir, oh yes Sir...that lady?...okay I'll meet her in your presence Sir, certainly...we require such technical experts in our surveillance Sir okay Sir!" Vinay concluded the conversation with a big relief and looked at Raghu with a smile in his face.

"So we have only two hours of time to start...has food parcel arrived?", Vinay asked him

"Yes Sir.....let's have it first...I'm damn hungry", Raghu got up.

They sat for lunch in the next room where the constables in his team got ready the lunch with chicken biryani with side dishes.

"Why non-veg now?...it would be heavy...isn't it?", Vinay asked Raghu.

"It's a token celebration on this breakthrough Sir...we should satisfy our mind and body on each and every small occasion that's for celebration Sir", Raghu tried to justify the items brought for lunch.

"One more thing Raghu....ACP Sir told about a lady who's expert in tracking technology.. and Sir said that she is expert in forensic psychology too...she's part of a team who got trained under the supervision of NIA...the team has arrived to our city two days ago...this lady....I don't know her name....she is said to be ready to offer her help in tracing and tracking the drug supplies into the city...so we're going to meet her when we'll meet ACP Sir...he said that he's arranging a meeting with her ...get ready with all the information and you should tell all your doubts before her! Be careful, she's from NIA! Okay? See technology has brought so much change in the working of the department!...isn't it?" Vinay concluded the phone briefing while enjoying the chicken biryani.

"That's wonderful Sir...yes Sir... we should need such technical support Sir...then it would be easy for us to control these buggers Sir...moreover...we can check mate the drug trafficking into the city Sir", Raghu responded visualizing the future appreciation he's going to get with the success of this operation.

He didn't expect that the lead in this case would fetch quick results so soon. He knew how hard his team has strived for the last three months to track the drug traffickers who are roaming so easily and turning the youth of the city into addicts to heroin and other narcotic drugs.

They finished their lunch quickly and while they are moving to ACP office, Raghu received a call in his mobile.

"Good news Sir!...our men located his house!...he's inside his house now....they asked for extra manpower to nab him once he comes out...we should send at least three constables Sir..!" Raghu looked at his boss with a broad smile and additional enthusiasm.

"Good!...send them immediately...send sub-inspector Vikram also...he's young and can run well in case a chase is needed...and one more thing...tell them to keep it like a petty case...no extra noise or no extra show of power...should finish the task smoothly...okay?", Vinay ordered while settling down in the front seat of his vehicle. As all the positive things are sequencing into his way, his confidence is in the ascending mode.

****

Rahul got down from the Auto near a commercial complex. He changed his attire into a youngster working in a small private company. A cloth bag containing the stuff is hanging on his right shoulder. He looked at his mobile. It is 3.00 PM. He has to deliver the big packet here. He already told the core member who was supposed to deliver the packet to a customer who is a partner of a pub located in the outskirts of the city. But the stuff should be delivered at this commercial complex. The core member informed Rahul that someone would come and collect the packet.

Rahul came to the entrance of the complex after ensuring that he was not under the coverage of any CC cameras. He made a call to the number given by the core member.

"Hello! Who is this?", someone responded.

"I'm waiting for the payment bro", Rahul used the code words told by the core member.

"Wait a minute...coming down", the call cut off.

Rahul waited for ten minutes. None came. He looked upwards. No indication of anyone looking down for him. It is a medium sized five storied commercial complex. The ground floor is occupied by a garments show room and a mobile shop along with a small restaurant at the corner side of the building. The above three floors are offices of private firms. The top floor seems being used for residential flats.

Rahul turned impatient. He looked around to see if anyone was waiting for him. He observed at the restaurant that someone was observing him keenly. Rahul casually diverted his looks from that person.

'Who's that watching at me?...police or their informer?', Rahul is thinking while looking around to find if anyone came for him.

As none is looking at him, he again looked at the person who watched him standing in front of the restaurant. That person is still watching him. Rahul started sweating.

'Must be informer!', he got frightened.

'Better I should leave from here', Rahul decided wiping the sweating from his fore head.

He could hear his heart beat clearly. Just before leaving the place, Rahul causally looked again at him. Suddenly, that person gave a slight signal by moving his head. Rahul stopped and looked at him again. He is indicating Rahul to come towards him. Rahul was puzzled.

'Who is he?...why is he signaling to come over there?', Rahul slowly moved towards him though he is not fully decided what to do. But before Rahul reaching him, he stood up and moved towards a lane behind the restaurant.

'So he must be the person whom I should deliver the stuff!', Rahul felt relieved of his tension.

Rahul reached the restaurant and after waiting for a while he entered the lane. That person was standing in the middle of the lane. Rahul reached him.

He looked scared. He is a well-dressed man aged about fifty years. As soon as Rahul reached him, he suddenly pulled out a cover from his pocket.

"Do as written down in this", he put the cover in Rahul's hand and swiftly moved towards other end of the lane and disappeared by turning into other road.

Rahul could not understand what is going on. He looked at the cover. It is a plastic cover folded around. He opened it. There are some bundles of currency notes along with a folded paper. He opened the paper. Some thing was scribbled on it.

'We have got the information. This area is under police surveillance. Take the payment and arrange for delivery the stuff at the pub tomorrow morning. Not today. Tomorrow the pub will be closed. The stuff must be reached by tomorrow evening. A person will be waiting inside the pub for you. Take precautions', Rahul read it amid increasing heartbeat.

He looked around. The lane was empty. It was around 4.00 PM. He looked at the currency. There are five bundles of five hundred notes.

'Two lakh and fifty thousand rupees...so payment has been made before delivery', Rahul thought.

He looked at the address given below. It is the pub for which the drug was supposed to be reached and got consumed by the customers.

Rahul sighed with a disappointment that though payment was received, he could not get rid of the stuff. He felt the shoulder bag heavier. He slowly came out of the lane carefully adjusting his bag hanging from his shoulder. He quickly entered the restaurant and ordered for tea settling down in a chair. He looked around. The evening crowd is scanty. None is looked suspicious. He finished the tea hurriedly and came out. On standing next to the pan shop located in front of the restaurant, Rahul lit a cigarette and started to scan the area with a casual but cautious glance. On the opposite side of complex, he spotted a person sitting in small café which is exactly opposite to the commercial complex building. That person is keeping an eye on the movements of people in and out of commercial complex. Particularly, he is looking upwards and observing the movements of persons from the top floors of the building.

Now, Rahul realized that because of him, the pub agent avoided to contact him directly. After a thorough second round of scanning, Rahul ensured that only one person is engaged to keep surveillance of the building.

'He must be an informer', Rahul decided based on his physical form.

He is lean and short. Rahul sighed in relief and slowly moved backward and covered himself behind some persons who are standing in front of the pan shop. Rahul wanted to wait for some more time there because, if he makes any small movement to leave the place, he will throw himself into the risk of being spotted by that person. Rahul slowly slid his shoulder bag onto the floor and pushed it with his foot to the back side of the pan shop. He purchased a cigarette pack in the pan shop and lit a cigarette.

While he is doing the counter surveillance, a police vehicle came there. It stopped near the café where the informer is sitting. That person stood up slowly and approached the vehicle. Rahul saw him standing in front of the driver of the vehicle and talking to police sitting inside the vehicle. As his attention was diverted, Rahul threw away the cigarette and quickly took his bag from where he kept it. He briskly walked towards the restaurant and from there slipped into the lane where he had received the cover. Once entered into the lane, Rahul ran towards the other end of the road. On reaching the main road where the lane path ended, he got into an auto.

'Somehow escaped from the scene!...but this stuff must be got rid of', Rahul wiped the sweating on his face.

He felt tired. He looked at his mobile. The time is 4.50 PM.

'The big packet is having time till tomorrow, now I should dispose of these sachets', Rahul checked in Google for the spot of the meeting where sachets are to be delivered.

'Five kilometers from here...that means around fifteen minutes...should reach there by 5.15 PM', Rahul assessed the position.

He got down the auto and after walking a while, called another auto and got in. It took half an hour to reach the area as the evening traffic is in the rising mode.

It is a godown. But the traffic is scanty in the area with lesser movement of people and vehicles. He moved towards the godown. He checked for cameras. There is only one on the right side of the godown. It is a food grains storing godown. The gate is ajar. None is there in front of the gate. There is a corridor path leading to godown building with fencing on both sides with full of bushes and gardening inside the fencing. He entered the corridor and moved towards the godown building. Suddenly, he heard the sound of claps. Rahul looked towards his left. Three persons are standing in front of a small building which must be the office of the godown. As Rahul approached them, one person came forward. He looked like a street rowdy with a big golden chain in his neck and a big metal bracelet to his left wrist. On approaching him, Rahul smelled that he is drunk.

"Why so late?...we are waiting for more than an hour...where are the packets?....You must be new...better maintain time schedule", that person scolded Rahul.

Rahul felt annoyed as he never experienced such a treatment from customers when he worked as delivery boy. But he did not talk anything and pulled out from his shoulder bag a plastic packet containing the sachets. The person grabbed the packet from Rahul's hand forcibly and counted the sachets.

"Yes....fifteen...okay...move out of here", the drunken man dictated Rahul.

"Money?", Rahul raised his voice.

He is fully tired and wanted to get rid of the stuff as quickly as possible.

"What money?...he took away the money in the morning itself...now move out of here!", the drunken man moved towards door as someone is impatiently calling him from inside.

Rahul looked at the window. Several persons are sitting there and some of them with glasses in their hands.

Rahul suppressed his anger and came out of the building as he could dispose the sachets at last. He made a call to the delivery boy. Voice message is telling that the phone is switched off.

Rahul realized that the delivery fellow who was appointed by Jack must have gone underground like Jack himself or quit the job as he was afraid of the increased surveillance of police after the news making rounds in the news channels. That is why he took the money and disappeared.

Rahul came out of the gate. It already became dark as very few street lights are on. He stopped near the bus stop and lit a cigarette. A person who is walking along the pavement, stopped at the bus stop and sat down on one of the metal chairs in the bus stop. Rahul looked at him casually. Suddenly, that person saw towards Rahul and jumped off the chair and tried to run from the place. But, Rahul moved quickly and caught hold of his hand firmly. He tried to remove himself of Rahul's hold in vain. Rahul recognized that he is the bald man whom Jack removed after he was tracked and searched by police a few months back.

"Why are you here?....where have been all these days?", Rahul asked being surprised of his unexpected appearance.

"I joined with other group...doing the same job there also", the bald man replied after ensuring that he could not escape from there.

Actually, he had been very friendly with Rahul when both were working together. They had involved in smooth delivery of hundreds of stuff packets with the mutual understanding developed between them. After that incident, suddenly he was kept aside and since then he has not been visible all these days.

"What?...other group?...where's it?...who runs it?", Rahul asked while his surprise is turning into shock.

He didn't expect such answer from him. This is a shocking revelation.

The bald man looked around. The area is poorly lit with scanty lighting of street lights here and there. He looked at Rahul. On looking into his eyes, Rahul loosened his grip on his hand. He sat down on a chair. Rahul is still standing and looking at him.

"After that when I was tracked by police on that day, Jack ordered me to leave the set up as I was proved unfit for the job...Actually, I was badly in need of money...I begged him not to remove from the job...first he didn't listen...but, that night I got a call from him...he wanted me to meet him immediately.", he stopped a while to take breathe.

Rahul is looking at him holding his breath.

"I met him that night...he engaged me in this job...same job...but for another group.... first I couldn't understand the existence of any other group as Jack is already leading this group....then he told me that the new group has more powerful political support and the existing group will become a scape goat for covering the new group and to mislead the police surveillance...many old delivery boys have been selectively chosen for working in the new group....you're still working in the old group...and now became even core member...I know one thing...he wanted me to keep it a top secret...particularly, you should not know that there's another group started to work under the control of Jack with new top bosses", bald man stopped again and looked at him.

Rahul is now in the real shock on listening what the bald man told like narrating a story. He could not speak anything immediately. He could not understand why he was kept in dark about a new set up running along. While he is thinking, the bald man stood up as if nothing is there to disclose.

"I'm going...actually...I'm going home after delivering the stuff in the fourth line of this street...I stopped here to catch a city bus...I was also surprised to see you here...I think you must be on your job...be careful...it's going to be more dangerous for the old group...I told this because...I like your way of working...I like the way you've grown up in the group within a few months...it was amazing...please keep it between us...bye", the bald man concluded and moved to other side of the road where he got into an auto.

Rahul's mind is blank. For a while, his mind stopped working. A city bus came and stopped in the stop. As he did not get in, it left. He is still standing alone there. His hand mechanically searched in the pocket for cigarette packet. He lit a cigarette. Slowly, his mind began to work. Rahul is now thinking.

'I entered the field after undergoing a lot of mental stress and after putting a lot of thought into it...after having weighed all the pros and cons.... and moreover....at that time I was left with no other better option...somehow I liked it because...it's fetching good income...that I have never seen my life.... but once settled down and working very hard in this setup.. and....after putting so much effort to grow up in the group...why now things are turning against me?...Why Jack turned against me?... he brought me into this... now he pushed me into the dangerous corner ...but why? I worked very hard for the organization...and with my efforts and plans as core member...the supplies have increased...earnings have increased and network has also increased with number of delivery boys also increased at a rapid pace....while I've started to enjoy my life...again it turned against me...why?', Rahul's mind is brewing with a lot of questions swirling in it without finding answers.

Rahul suddenly came into his senses as a police vehicle came into the street. His heart started to beat rapidly. The big stuff packet is still in his sling bag. Rahul stood there like a passenger and casually lit another cigarette. The vehicle moved ahead without stopping there. He sighed in relief. After the police vehicle disappeared from his sight, Rahul threw away the cigarette and crossed the road to stop an auto.

*****

"Damn it Raghu!...how that bastard escaped from our team?....it is shameful!...what can I tell ACP Sir about this?...should I tell that our efficient team was sleeping while that guy escaped walking in front of them?" Vinay is furious and frustrated when Raghu received a call from the team.

The team has just now informed him that when they entered the suspect's house, he already disappeared through the back side window of his bed room. None was there in his house.

Vinay felt much anguished over the information. Last evening both of them met the ACP and narrated to him about the lengthy plans they are going to implement to bust the drug trafficking mafia which is rapidly expanding its activities to the nook and corner of the city.

Raghu is standing in front of his table with the clear disappointment writ large on his face. He made a call to the team to collect all the useful evidences from the house.

"What shall we do there if nothing is available?...he could smell them....that's why he could escape so smartly.....it's foolish that he could leave any useful evidence from his house!", Vinay is still furious but quickly came into his senses.

"Sir, since the delivery man has escaped...let's hope for the useful information if anything available there... it is now the boy who received the packets from him is the only source of evidence for us...we have to interrogate him...but, it's not so easy to take him into custody...ACP Sir has already told that we should be careful in dealing the case from the boy's side keeping in view the clout and influence his father has in political circles", Raghu tried to make his boss to get out of the frustration.

"What's the news from Suneel?...the boy went to school today?", Vinay asked him thinking that it would be better to focus the issue from the boy's side.

"Yes Sir, got the info from him...he is there in the school", Raghu felt some relief as his boss has got back into the usual business.

Vinay thought for a while about handling the boy to get any information about the stuff receipts.

'Now teenagers are so smart...not easily yielding to our techniques', Vinay is thinking.

Suddenly, he looked at Raghu with flashing eyes.

"Why shouldn't we give this to that tracking experts? they can handle it smoothly...particularly that the tracking team leader you know... she gave us so many inputs about the collection of information if the delivery man is caught!", Vinay waited for his response.

"Good idea Sir!...she can handle the boy very well...instead of us it would be safe if she or her team deals from that side...so no headache from political circles!", Raghu endorsed the idea recollecting the beautiful face of the lady track expert.

"Let's be silent about the guy escaped...already I got the permission for going ahead in approaching the boy...bring the details of the boy...I'll talk to her", Vinay ordered with some relief as he is able to make plan B.

Raghu forwarded the details of the boy to Vinay.

*****

Rahul is walking along the rural road in the outskirt of the city. As it is around twenty five kilometers from city limits, Rahul came by auto upto cross road that leads to the pub. There he got down from the auto and after sending the auto, he waited there for a while and after ensuring that the auto is out of sight, started walking towards the pub which is located at more than two kilometers from there. The time is around 10.00 AM. The sun is very bright. The rural traffic is scanty with one or two bikes going towards the city from the adjacent villages. The narrow road is covered with small bushes and trees on both sides. Beyond them, the area is spread with paddy fields. After walking for half an hour, he sighted the pub building. It is built in an extent of about two acres with a compound wall on the front side and wire fencing all the other side. There is a sign board on the top of the building. Its name is Dim 'n' Din.

On reaching the gate, he stood there for a while and looked inside wiping the sweat on his face. He didn't find any sign of movement of persons inside. He looked around if any watchman is there. Actually, as per the slip, he should handover the stuff to somebody here. As he is not having any contact details of the person to whom it is to be delivered, Rahul entered inside the premises. There is a lot of space for car parking. Two cars are being parked at the right side corner. But nobody is seen there. He reached the entrance of the pub building. First room is like a small drawing room with a lot of chairs. From there he entered the next door that is ajar. He opened the door. It is a corridor which is leading to two doors. He reached the first door. It is locked. The second door is open with fully draped curtains. He entered through the curtains. It is the main hall of the pub. Rahul knows about pubs as he worked in pubs also. None is there. He looked around. There is a back side door. He went to it. It is leading to back yard where toilets are there in a row. He came back again into the main hall. There are four rooms on the right side of the hall.

'Why nobody is there....whom should I deliver this?", Rahul is getting irritated as he is in hurry to get rid of the stuff from his possession.

"Hello!...is anybody there?", Rahul shouted.

"Who is it?", a male voice came from first room.

Rahul went to there and opened the door. He found three persons in their thirties lying on the bed. They appeared as if they were boozing throughout last night. They are lying like logs on the bed. Lot of bottles are scattered on the tea table and on the side table of the big size bed. One person slowly got up and looked at Rahul.

"Who are you?", he asked Rahul with sleepy eyes.

His eyes are red as he didn't sleep last night.

"I came for delivering this", Rahul told him showing the stuff cover taken out from his shoulder bag.

"Oh you!....yes...I got a call last night...waiting for you...you should have come last night....many customers went back as the stock got exhausted...okay...keep it there and go away...don't stay here...close the door and go!", He fell back on the bed again.

Suddenly, one of the persons lying on the bed got up like a spring and yelled, "Give it to me...I'm waiting for it.....last night there's no stuff...Give it to me", he extending his hand.

Rahul is surprised. That guy is a teenager. Perhaps he may be around fifteen years old.

'The stuff's already reached the kids!', Rahul wondered.

He kept the stuff packet on the bed side table and came out of the room without responding to the teenager's begging for the packet.

Rahul stood there for a while and sighed in relief as he has disposed the stock. Then he came in to the hall and moved towards corridor without looking back.

'Better to leave the place as soon as possible', he thought.

Suddenly, he heard a faint voice from the next room. He stopped there. He touched the door. It's not bolted inside. He pushed the door. It is also similar to the first one with a king size bed. A female probably in her early twenties is lying on the bed nakedly. She is in semi-conscious state and making slight movements.

"Give me just a pinch please....I'm dying....just give me a pinch of my powder please!", she is moaning.

Rahul quickly came out of the room and closed the door. He rushed towards the door as his mouth is getting dried.

'What's the hell is going on here!', he was shocked and cursed himself on coming here for delivery of the stuff.

Rahul briskly moved out of the building wiping off the sweat around his neck that is pouring down his body as if he has just now finished a running race.

As he came out of the gate, he saw a police vehicle coming towards the building. Rahul got frightened. He quickly moved towards the right side of the building and ran towards the bushes and jackfruit trees behind the building. While running, he looked back and got more frightened as the police vehicle is coming towards his direction. He started to run fast and reached the bushy area where there is no proper way to any vehicle to move into the thick bushes. But Rahul realized that police saw him and started to chase him. He kept on running for the next few minutes till he reached a small road leading to rural areas.

He waited there for a while, gasping heavily. He looked back towards the bushes and found that there was no sign of police movement.

'They must have gone into the pub', Rahul thought and sighed in relief for escaping so narrowly from the police.

As he is thinking of which direction he should move now, he saw a local sharing auto coming from right side. It is fully packed. Rahul stopped the auto and adjusted himself on side plank besides the auto driver. As the auto moved, Rahul wiped the sweat around his neck and face and closed his eyes as he needed some rest.

****

CHAPTER THIRTEEN

"How low levels to these girls are stooping down? So shameless! Disgusting!", Vinay's wife, Padma's voice is reflecting her loathing while watching the breaking news in the morning itself.

Inspector Vinay is sitting in the living room in his house and watching the news while sipping the coffee served by his wife.

The female news reader is going on narrating about the police raiding on the pub with excellently added spices. She is all smiles while her eyes and lips are moving so dramatically for each phrase coming out of her mouth. She is telling step by step how police had caught the drug stuff along with the consumers. She is telling about each scene with a high pitched voice as if she was there during the raid. The visuals of the pub and the persons who were arrested are also being displayed scene by scene repeatedly. All the arrested are with masks over their heads.

"By the way....did you see that girl naked? Wasn't there any female constable while raiding the pub?", Padma raised a query looking at him sharply.

She maintained a low voice as their son is wrestling with the balance homework in the study room.

"No...No...Padma!...I didn't see her!...our constables immediately covered her with a bed sheet!...you know....I would be very careful in such a situation....later, our lady constables came and brought her to station....she wasn't fully conscious...you know!", Vinay shrugged his shoulders while patting himself in his mind for the talent in fabricating scenes instantaneously as and when required to tell her.

She's satisfied with his answer and went into the kitchen with the coffee cup emptied by him.

Vinay's thoughts went back to yesterday and onto the person who escaped so narrowly from the pub premises. As they were in a hurry to reach the pub, they could not even take a snap of that person. The persons who were taken into custody including that girl are under interrogation. They are being queried and examined by the police and also an expert team headed by the forensic psychologist. She has already gathered much information about the girl. The girl is of a middle class background and working in a small software company in the city. She became a drug addict because of her boyfriend who supplies her drug packets in exchange of her body offered for certain selective rich customers coming to the pub. Out of the other three members who were caught in the other rooms, one is a customer and the two are service boys working in the pub. Search is going on for her boyfriend.

'Who was that guy? He is not her boyfriend! because she's given his details and photos also....then who's this guy?...Pub owners have already surrendered...they're politically influential and are safe as far as their connection with drug supplies is concerned....they're claiming that they don't supply drugs to customers in the pub...The CCTV camara is working in the main hall of the pub....that too....the events were captured selectively by cleverly switching off and on the cameras....nowhere the person who ran towards the bushes was seen.....had he been caught, the story would have been more conclusive!', Vinay sighed disappointingly.

He is worried about the missing threads that are leaving the police a hapless lot in busting the mafia behind the drug racket that has been shaking the city.

Suddenly, his mobile started to ring. It is from Raghu. He received the call.

"Sir...we've got the backside CCTV footage of the Pub!...the scenes of that person who run away when we raided were also covered!", Raghu's voice is so loud and joyful as if he invented the camera itself.

"Is it!?....that's great!....how it was opened!", Vinay felt very happy on hearing the breaking news.

"It's been opened by forensic people Sir!....Forensic madam is studying the footage...Hope...she would find who he is!", Raghu's voice is so sweet to listen.

"I'll be there in twenty minutes.", Vinay switched of the mobile and rushed to bathroom.

****

Rahul suddenly woke up and looked around. Felt relieved as he found that he was lying on his bed.

'Why did I wake up so suddenly?', He thought for a while.

'Yes! It's a dream that made me to get up with a jerk', he felt relieved.

He tried to recollect the dream he was living in till a few moments ago. It was not clear where it started. But, he could recollect that he was running in a narrow lane to escape from somebody. He did not know who were chasing him. But, he was running as if he would certainly be killed if caught. He increased his speed hoping that he would escape from them. Though gasping, he was using his full strength to run as fast as he could. Suddenly, the road came to an end! There was no further way or lane to turn. It was dead end! He got panicked. He turned back to look for those who was chasing him. He found with a shiver in his back that someone rushed so close and almost started to attack him with a weapon! Then he woke up!

'Oh! What a dream!', Rahul sighed in relief that it happened in a dream.

He recollected the sequence of the events he experienced yesterday. After escaping from police and catching an auto, he got down and changed three autos and was moving around the city desperately till the evening. He reached home at around 10.00 PM in the night and fell down on his bed. He slipped into sleep while thinking what to do for escaping from police.

After finishing the recollecting process, Rahul got up from the bed and came into the balcony. It is 6.30 AM. He lit a cigarette and looked around. It is a bright morning. The view appeared as usual and normal.

'Yes....I had escaped from the police!...They couldn't find me because, they saw me behind that pub located in the outskirts of the city....that too almost in the opposite direction from my residence...The distance must be around seventy kilometers!' , He felt more confident now.

'What to do now!', Rahul started to think for the next course of action.

'Now I'm not having any stock in my possession....I could rid of everything.....I should work for wiping off all the evidences of my connections with drug mafia and delivery chain!'...but, how to do that?', he is thinking but could not find any striking answer.

Rahul came into the kitchen to prepare some coffee as he felt hungry. He has not taken food since yesterday morning except a tea and a couple of samosas at some junction point while changing autos.

He came back to the balcony with the coffee cup.

'I should not use this dress again...I should destroy it...I should not go nearer to the pub area....at least five kilometers around the pub area.....Yes...that would be safe....and urgently, I need to change my hair style....keep slight beard....that would be enough for a changed look...Yes!', His thoughts are going in full swing as he kept sipping hot block coffee.

The process is gaining some new confidence in him. He took a cigarette from the pack and searched for the lighter in his pocket. While lighting the cigarette, he heard the ringing sound of his mobile from the bed room where he left the mobile. He went to the bed room. It is still ringing. It is a new number. He looked at the time. It is 7.30 AM.

'Who is this?...calling so early in the morning!', Rahul thought for a while and decided to receive it.

"Hello!", His voice is cautious.

"Immediately leave the city...otherwise...you'll be in great trouble...police are searching for you!", the voice is new to Rahul.

He never talked to that person. It is a new number and new voice.

"Who are you?", Rahul asked interrupting the person by suppressing the pressure mounting in his mind.

His thoughts are squirreling aimlessly to all angles to find who is this guy? And why is threatening me?

"Shut up! Do what's said!", the call went off.

The voice was so commanding and curtly.

Rahul stood there like an erected log for a few seconds as his mouth getting dried.

'It must be from the mafia!, yes... they must have got the tip that I was seen and escaped from the police!', Rahul swallowed the gulp generated in the mouth.

'What to do now?,,, if they are worried.... It means....police must be on the hunt for me!', he felt the sudden tingle in his back.

Earlier, he has experiences of escaping from police without being identified by them. But, they are looking for him.

'Did they recognize me?', Rahul got a new doubt.

'Yes!....I must've been recognized!...otherwise...I wouldn't receive such calls from the mafia side', this new thought made his heart thumping vigorously. Now he could listen it.

Suddenly, Rahul searched his mobile and tried to make calls to Jack. He is having two or three numbers. Two numbers replied that the mobile was switched off. He tried for the recent number on which he received a call from Jack. After sometime, he could identify the number. Rahul held his breath as the number is ringing.

"You bloody idiot....why are you making calls?....I told you run off immediately...both police and they are after you", Jack's voice is hoarse as usual but sounded irritated.

"Thanks Jack for responding....but who are they?", Rahul's voice is fumbling with a mixed feeling of angst and fear.

"It's...another group...more powerful...the old one was already disbanded...these people are dangerous too...they knew that police are coming so close....I think you're seen...that's why the new group is after you...we're in danger...run off idiot... don't make calls to me", the call went off abruptly.

'So....it's confirmed!...there is another group!...Jack worked for both...I was also working for both the groups without knowing who were there!...', Rahul's mind got the conclusion.

****

"See this Sir, while we're entering into the scene, that man started running towards backside of the pub", Raghu explained the scene captured in the CCTV footage of the pub.

Vinay keenly watched the footage. A young man with blue jeans and white shirt is racing towards the bushes without looking back and soon disappeared into the bushes located at a distance of hundred meters from the pub. He is tall and strong.

'Must be around twenty five years old', Vinay thought looking at the footage again and again.

"Has Sheela Madam team watched it?" , He asked Raghu.

"Yes Sir!...She watched it several times and studying it since the morning in her laptop...She would brief you soon I think Sir" Raghu said.

Before he completed his words, Sheela entered the CI's cabin with her team mates.

She is in blue jeans topped with a black striped white salwar kameez. The laptop bag is hanging on her shoulder. She carried two big folder files with her. The two members who are in her team, a young lady and young man in their early twenties, wished Vinay with a broad smile.

"Good morning Sir!" Sheela wished.

"Very Good morning Madam! .... at last, we got some footage which may lead us forward....What's your point?", Vinay looked at her curiously.

"Call me Sheela Sir! No formalities please!", She smiled.

He likes her as an excellent hand for the department in various angles. She works in the spheres of forensics, criminal psychology, clue findings and also cyber related frauds and crimes. He wonders her knowledge of the subjects and accurate conclusions in the tasks assigned. Soon after joining the department as an outsourced aide, she has become an inevitable hand for almost all the cases handled by him. She works and extends her services in all the zones in the City.

"Yes Sir! The footage is really a breakthrough for us!.We're working on it. Once, the person's identity is established, we can certainly move forward in finding the mafia behind it. That's certain!", Sheela replied in a firm and serious tone.

"Is it!...well!...then it's a cheerful news for us! Why do you look so serious? Have the tea!", Vinay offered tea while sipping tea in his cup.

"Thanks Sir! But we need to study the footage covering various aspects related with the case Sir! Then only, I would come up with my findings....my request is please leave this task to our team...we have to examine it without any others involvement please!" Sheela asked him with a requesting voice.

"Wow...that's interesting! if you're so interested, why not?...okay do this! but the task should be completed with a good result and without wasting our time! Okay?", Vinay responded with the satisfaction that she requested him so obediently.

He knows that even ACPs talk to her in a polite way while dealing tough cases. He witnessed such scenes several times within last six months.

'She stands as the best example for the caption Beauty with Brains', Vinay thought while watching her.

"Thanks a lot Sir!", Sheela stood up and moved out with her team.

As soon as Sheela left his cabin, Vinay made a call to the ACP Bhargav and briefed the status of the case.

"Sheela madam will come up with accurate findings Sir...I hope we're going to find who are behind it soon!", Raghu said after Vinay finished his briefing.

"Yes Raghu....I'm also fully confident...certainly she'll find a way for us to move forward...let's see...and by the way...ACP Sir wanted notes for press meet on the pub raid...have you got the papers ready...first do that ...we have to submit them by the evening. Okay?", Vinay ordered.

****

Rahul slowly came onto the road from behind the compound wall of a house where he was hiding for the last half an hour. It is a small house in a middle class locality. It seems no one was there in the house as it is locked. Perhaps the residents must have left home on a tour at least a week ago. The premises is dusty and covered with the dry leaves fallen from the mango and guava trees inside the compound wall. He jumped into the compound wall when a police jeep came into the street. As the jeep stopped a few metres away from the house and the police were appeared watching the area keenly, he was sitting behind the compound wall till now. After the jeep left, he waited there for another fifteen minutes and after ensuring that the jeep would not come back, he came out. As the time is around 3.30 PM, no movement was there in the residential locality.

He left his flat two days ago. When he had spoken to Jack the last time he confirmed that the other group of the mafia working in the field was more strong and ruthless as it has the political support also. So he thought it would not be safe residing in the flat because they could have already traced his location. After wandering outside for two days here and there, he dicided to return to his flat as he did not know what to do.

'Better to move to somewhere else...but where to go...where to stay...and how long?', Rahul is clueless about the future course of action.

'All these days, I have been leading the life as the busiest person in supply of heroin and earning income. I have enjoyed the new life style since I joined the field', His thoughts are continuing while he is lying on his bed.

Suddenly, Rahul came into the present with the doorbell sound. He is startled with doorbell sound.

'Who's that?...at this time?', he wondered.

He looked through the peephole. It is security guard of the gated community. Rahul opened the door. He knows him.

"Good afternoon Sir....Sorry for the disturbance...yesterday evening when you left the flat, some people came and asked about your flat Sir....I forgot to tell you yesterday as I was leaving the duty" the Security guard told politely.

"Who're they?...how many of them came?" Rahul's heart beat increased.

"Four young men Sir....out of them one was foreigner! Seems a Nigeria man. I mean a black guy...they insisted to meet you since they came on urgent work....I told them that you're not in the flat....they enquired about the flat number and went away...we asked them to leave a mobile number so as to inform later...but they left without responding", he replied in detail.

"Okay...I'll find who they are...no problem...by the way, if they come again in my absence, please call me...but...not in their presence....Okay?", Rahul looked at him putting a hundred rupees note in his shirt pocket.

"Okay Sir...thanks Sir", the Security guard went away with a broad smile.

Rahul closed the door and sank into sofa in the drawing room.

'Who were they? ... one was black...means Jack?...No, Jack certainly will not come....they must be from the second group!...that means...they narrowed down on my location!...Oh!...I'm in real danger!...What Jack alerted me is right!...they are tracking me!....they will certainly come again...they must be watching me from somewhere near the gated community!', Rahul's heart is pounding with rapid beats.

'I should immediately run away from here', Rahul stood up and went inside.

He stuffed a few clothes and casuals in the bag. He opened the table drawer and started counting the money.

'One lakh and twenty four thousand rupees left with me...very less...how to survive with this amount?', He was disappointed with the money left with him.

He put ten thousand rupees in his wallet and kept the remaining amount in the bag. He looked at the watch. It is around 5.30 PM in the evening. Rahul locked the flat main door and went down. The same security guard is on duty. He came towards Rahul.

"Are you going out Sir? .... I'll call you if they come again", he told in low voice as if Rahul is leaving the premises so urgently just to avoid a meeting with them.

"Yes...I'm going out on some urgent work...you do one thing...if they come again, tell them that I hadn't turn up since their last visit...please don't forget...Okay?", Rahul also replied in low voice to match with the tone of the security guard.

"Okay Sir...I'll tell them so....even if they come in my absence...I'll brief the next man on duty to tell them exactly what you said!", he replied in equally matching tone as if he has been elevated as his close confidant.

Rahul left the premises and looked around just to find whether anyone is watching or hiding somewhere for him. Fortunately, the road is desolated with scanty traffic. No car or any other vehicle is seen parked in the vicinity. Rahul sighed in relief and called an auto parked near to him. He wanted to move to some ordinary hotel far away from his residence so that they could not be in a position to trace his whereabouts. He searched in his mobile about cheaper hotels nearer to his earlier residence where he resided before entering the field.

"Go to Omega hotel", Rahul told the driver while getting into the auto.

'Yes...that area would be far away from the present residence....almost twenty five kilometers from here...it's quite funny!...or surprising rather...I'm going back to the starting point!', Rahul thoughts slowly went back to his movements where he lived just about a year ago.

Auto started and his thoughts are running along.

Suddenly, he thought of Imran!

'I didn't know how he is? ... He must be busy as usual with his work and striving hard for the family once he gets married...oh! I forgot when his marriage would take place...I changed my SIM...now no more calls could be received from him....anyway, I should avoid calling him now...it would be very dangerous for Imran too if I try to contact him', Rahul sighed while a depressive mood set in to cover his mind.

As the traffic has slowly become heavy and the evening is turning into dark with the winter season, auto is moving slowly.

Rahul looked at his watch. It's almost 7.00 PM.

'It took more than one hour to reach here', Rahul thought while getting down near Omega hotel.

Omega hotel looked like a timeless memorial. The same lights ... the same buzz of evening crowd.....the same high pitched yells and screams. Rahul slowly entered the hotel and ordered for an *Irani tea*. It took him ten minutes to get his cup. He stood at the regular and favourite place. The smell and the taste of the tea are nostalgic and brought back memories of his attachment with the hotel.

He finished the tea and came out. The City Central Station is brimming with regular crowd and vehicular movement. Rahul lit a cigarette. He looked around to select a suitable one out of the many lodges located around Omega hotel. After finishing his cigarette, he moved towards an old lodge located on the left side.

He took a Non-AC room in the second floor. The room service boy took him to the room and left after keeping the bag on the table and receing the tip. Rahul looked around the room. It consists of a single bed with attached small bathroom, a small table, chair and a wall mounted TV set. There is a window next to bathroom. Rahul opened the bag. He brought only some casuals and a towel. He took out the charger from the side pocket of the bag and kept the mobile on charging. He sat down on the bed drinking water from the bottle kept on the table. He opened the window and lit a cigarette. The time is around 8.00 PM. Night traffic of the city is seen from the window.

'Now I'm away from my residence and moved to this room far away....but...don't know what to do...nothing is striking', Rahul felt his mind is vacillating.

'Better to go down and eat something', Rahul moved into bathroom.

He is hungry as he hasn't taken anything since the morning. After getting bath and changing his casuals, he went down straightly to Omega hotel. After having a plate of parotas with egg curry, he crossed the road and purchased two packs of cigarettes, tooth paste and a brush. He wanted to stay in the lodge at least for a week so that the din rising over the pub raid would get diminished. Particularly, on the electronic and print media.

Rahul came back to room and lit a cigarette. After having satiated his hunger, now his mind is working.

He took the remote and switched on the TV. He changed to news channels to know whether there is any news is going on drugs or pub raid. Nothing is interesting. While changing the channels, he suddenly stopped at a local news channel where a news story related with drug culture is going on. Rahul kept the remote on the bed and started to watch it. The anchor is telling how heroin is being smuggled into the city, how it is being reached to final consumption in various forms like small packets, injections, cigarettes and even as chocolates or small size candies. Colleges and schools became main target for the sale of the drug. At a school one student was shown caught while bringing a heroin chocolates into school. Consumption in pubs and private parties is rampant. Youth is fast getting addicted to it. Particularly, young and teenage girls are falling prey to it. Once addicted, they are becoming toys in the hands of the boyfriends or suppliers who are exploiting them sexually. Because of their addiction, girls are allowing the exploitation and becoming silent victims. In two cases, girls in teenage committed suicide as they could not bear the continuous exploitation and fear of family knowing about what they were doing. In one more case, a young boy was attacked by his classmates for disclosing to their principal that they were consuming drugs. The boy was brutally beaten and is now in ICU in a critical condition. Certain sections of police and some political big shots are working hand in glove with drug mafia. Because of their support, the drug mafia unleashed the drug culture in all the corners of this big city and is spreading to adjacent urban and rural areas too. The mafia business is roughly estimated by the police at around nine hundred crore rupees per year. The city has become a drug hub for smuggling, processing and distribution of heroin to other states too. The state and central governments are forced to look into the alarming situation that is becoming worse day by day. The anchor narrated the story with apt illustrations of suitable clippings at right points. He even touched the point that how poor and unemployed youngsters particularly, girls are being dragged in to the mafia net exploited as drug suppliers to the end users. At the end of the story there was a small interview of an ACP rank police officer who stated that they were striving hard for nabbing the bigwigs behind the mafia. He told that a foreigner by name Jack was crucial in the mafia and was narrowly escaped from the police but he is still within the City limits. The officer appealed to the public to come forward and cooperate with police in fighting against the drug mafia and eradicating the drug culture from this most happening city. Then two more persons, one belonging to a political party another one from a civil liberties society spoke and vehemently blamed the governments on their failure in controlling the drug supplies into the city. There ended the story.

Rahul's throat got dried up. It is a twenty minutes story told without any interruption of commercial breaks. He switched off the TV once the story was over. He took the water bottle and emptied it. He never expected that the field in which he was working was so dangerous and so bad against the people of the city. He was shocked on seeing that how youth is getting spoiled and losing their lives by getting crippled in the iron net of the drug mafia.

'So Jack was already identified by the police! He can't escape...situation has become so worse!', Rahul could listen his heartbeat.

Sweating started oozing from the sides of his ears. He could sense that he is slightly shivering. For the first time, he is feeling very bad about the job he was doing for the last one year. When Jack offered the job, he was frightened that it was a bad thing. But he was nicely trapped and dragged into this hell's net with a temptation of getting a good life.

'Yes... it's given me good life which I couldn't afford earlier....but at the cost of unpardonable harm to the young generation...yes... that's too bad!... I've committed a big crime! ... I'm a criminal!", Rahul's eyes are cascading with tears.

He chided himself as to why he could not think this way while accepting the job. Rahul is lying on the bed looking at the ceiling for a long time. Suddenly, he got up and sat down.

'If this is bad against so many youngsters like me, I shouldn't indulge in it.... I should come out and fight against it...that's the right thing I can do! Let police arrest me! ... Better to be in jail than hiding away like this!', Rahul felt a spreading relief in his mind.

He took out his mobile and rang up to Imran's number. It is ringing but Imran did not lift. He wanted to share his feelings with Imran. Because there is none other than Imran to rekindle his morale at this pathetic situation. Imran knows everything about him.

'He is the only hope for me through whom I can approach police and help them curtailing the mafia', Rahul's mind is running fast in forming a final decision on the next course of action.

He tried three more times to contact Imran but, no use.

'He is not lifting....yes, it's a new a number... he is more cautious of responding to unknown numbers.... Imran must've contacted to my original number', Rahul got disappointed.

He wanted to hear Imran's voice and share his feelings and the critical position in which he is trapped in.

'Imran, this is Rahul.. I'm in a critical position...I want to talk to you...it is very urgent ... please call me back', Rahul sent a voice message to Imran through his whatsapp account.

Rahul stood up and went to the window and lit a cigarette. Now he feels having got some relief as there is someone who could share his feelings and extend support in this difficult phase.

While he is looking through the window, his mobile started to ring up. It's Imran!

'Yes!... once seen the message he will not waste a minute in responding', Rahul grabbed the phone.

"Imran!", Rahul's voice turned emotional.

"Yaar!...What happened?....Where are you?", Rahul could hear the concern in Imran's voice.

"My position is not good Imran!... I'm in trouble...drug mafia and police are after me....I committed a big blunder by entering the drug field...that's why I couldn't contact you all these days!", Rahul's voice got choked with the lump in his throat.

"My God!...what's you're talking about!! ...you... in the drug field!?...what a matter I'm hearing from you

Yaar!...first of all tell me what happened", Imran came into his senses.

He sensed that Rahul is in real danger. He never heard Rahul talking to him in such a meek and worrying tone. He realized that Rahul is badly in need of his support.

Rahul told Imran everything he has hidden from him for the last one year. For the next fifteen minutes, Imran attentively listened to him without any interruption.

"Rahul...don't worry, now you've realized your mistake and ready to confess before police. That's good and that's the only option before us! Don't be panic! You stay there in that lodge, I'll contact a lawyer there through my old contacts. It would be better to approach court through a lawyer than to directly surrender to police...isn't it? Don't make any calls to any one...I'll come back with full details of the next course of action. I'll be there by day after tomorrow...once I reached there, we'll contact the lawyer...Okay...be calm...please stay there. I think that would be a safe place for you...Bye Yaar!", Imran cut the call.

Rahul felt relieved. Till now he didn't know that he could approach a lawyer to become an approver before a court of law.

'Imran knows what's the right thing....had he been here I wouldn't have got trapped into this dangerous mafia net', Rahul sighed with diminishing distress.

****

CHAPTER FOURTEEN

"Sheela...why don't you come for lunch?...it's already two thirty!. Today it's Sunday! A holiday...why're you doing so much work?" Sheela's mother asked her coming into her room.

"I'm not hungry ma...I've so much work to do! Don't disturb me!" Sheela replied with a vexed voice on being called for lunch so many times.

Sheela is fully engaged with her laptop.

Her mother silently stood there for a while. She knows that when Sheela replied so, she shouldn't be disturbed. She slowly went back sighing about the way Sheela is leading her professional life. After getting into this job, there has been so much change in Sheela which she could not imagine.

She went to bedroom where Sheela's father Rama Rao is lying on the bed.

"Didn't she come for lunch?" Sheela's father asked with a dull voice. Her mother nodded in agreement.

"What happened to Baby?", he is anxious the way she is talking now a days.

"I don't know...after getting into this, she has become like that", Sheela's mother groaned while lying on the bed next to him. As it is a holiday, he is at home at this time.

Sheela's mother recollected what happened last night. Sheela had come home at around nine when her father was waiting for her. He had shown her a photograph of a handsome young man. He told her that he had brought her a wonderful match and this would be a very good proposal for marriage. The young man is an IT professional working in a big IT company in the city.

On seeing the photo, Sheela yelled at her father.

"I don't see any match...I'm not interested to marry now...how many times I've told you both...stop this harassment for a while!", Sheela told them in a raised voice filled with irritation as she was dashing into her room.

Since then, she has not come out of her room. She spent time looking into her laptop.

Her mother was surprised the way she talked to her father. She never spoke like that. In fact, Sheela is a father's kid. She is always more friendly with her father. She knows that her father worked so hard with a small job to bring up her. He never said no to whatever she wanted even with his limited income.

"Jaya, I think Baby is in love with some one!?..That's why she is talking like this?", Rama Rao looked at his wife thoughtfully.

Jaya looked into his eyes for a while. She too became suspicious about this. Sheela does not hide anything from parents. She shares every incident with her parents. But both of them have observed so much of change in her for the last two years and since she joined the job. They thought it normal since nowadays she is busy with her duty as she is working with police department.

"I don't know...if that be the case, she would certainly tell us or at least she would've told you" Jaya told in a low voice.

"Yes.....but she may be feeling shy about revealing that! Better you talk to her. She may tell the matter...If that is true, we can move forward... because she's a good girl and won't take any wrong step.....isn't it?" Rama Rao looked at her.

Jaya looked at him silently.

"Yes she must be in love with someone in the police department! I'll find out what's in her mind", She replied while turning to other side for taking a small snooze after lunch.

In the next room, Sheela is lying on the bed and looking at the laptop screen. She must have spent looking at the video clip running for more than fifty times since last night.

It is the footage of Rahul who was seen running off the pub premises. On seeing him in that long shot captured in the CCTV camera fixed in the backyard of the pub, she immediately identified him as Rahul. She can identify him in any angle. At the end of the clip while climbing the sloped mud bund filled with trees, he slightly looked back to ensure whether police were still chasing him. That angle is enough for Sheela to confirm that it is Rahul. He was a little stout than she had seen him last time and there was some change in his hairstyle. Earlier he used to maintain long curly hair almost covering his fore head. Now in this clip, he had a nice summer cut. After climbing up the slope, he vanished into the toddy palm trees and thickly grown bushes.

'Why Rahul? Why you came into this? What happened to you? Why this torture for me?' Sheela sighed in a soliloquial tone.

She was shocked when this clip was shown to her by the department personnel. Since then, she has not been able to digest that he is involved in this big mafia case. What puzzling her the most is that this field is not at all suitable for Rahul. He is an ordinary person who would like to work and earn from a petty job.

‘Certainly, he must have been trapped into this, Rahul would never indulge into this’, Sheela consoled herself.

‘Where is he now? How to trace him...atleast, I don’t have his mobile number. He is a lonely person....No friends circle! How to contact him!?’, Sheela’s mind is getting agonized.

While thinking vaguely about his whereabouts, suddenly it struck to her mind in a flash about a person whom she had seen along with Rahul twice.

Once, she saw him with Rahul at a hotel. He appeared so close to Rahul. The other time, she had seen both of them standing in front of a tailoring shop in the old city. She still remember that a tailor tape was hanging around the neck of the person.

“Yes!...he must be working in that shop!”, Sheela told herself openly. She decided to contact that person.

“Mummy...I’m taking lunch....I have to go to office urgently”, She yelled at her parents room and went into kitchen.

****

Rahul returned from Omega hotel after finishing a quick lunch. He lit a cigarette and started to think.

‘Nothing else I can do now except waiting for Imran’s arrival’, he thought firmly.

While he is brooding about the future course of action, his mobile started ringing. It’s an unknown number through whatsapp.

‘Who is this?’. Rahul turned suspicious and decided against lifting the call remembering what Imran told him.

But the number continued three more times. Rahul has become more suspicious. Suddenly, a whatsapp message appeared on the mobile screen. He looked at it. It is from the same number. After thinking for a while, he opened the message.

"I'm your old colleague...I want to talk to you...don't worry...I assure no harm from me", Rahul puzzled on reading the message.

While trying to recollect who this person is, Rahul made a whatsapp call to that number.

"Hello bro....I'm your old colleague...I think you're Rakesh...you know me", the person responded.

Rahul recognized his voice. He is the person who worked along with him in the old group. He was in his late thirties who used to be very cordial and friendly with Rahul while exchanging the stuff. But Rahul had never moved so closely to any one while attending his job.

"What's the matter?", Rahul asked him as his suspicion is rapidly going down.

"See Rakesh...we're, that means the persons like you and I who had worked along with Jack in the old group, are in danger....the new group is being run by powerful political backing...Since police have intensified the search operations, now the group wants to finish us!. They don't leave any evidence of the past...I'm leaving the city...I know you...you're a wrong person in this field....I know how you were trapped into this field by Jack", he is telling continuously with a sympathetic tone.

"What trap?...What Jack did to drag me into this?", Rahul interrupted his speech.

"Yes bro...you're not fired from the job in that mall...you know?...It's Jack's trap...actually the amount in your counter was stolen by Jack by distracting your attention!....I was also there at that time....Jack dragged many persons into this field playing such tricks...you know?", the person told in a steady voice.

Rahul felt shocked and could not speak.

"Listen bro...I think you're still moving in the city. Better leave the city immediately! Police are also looking after you...though you've successfully escaped from the pub raid, they saw you from the back! Since then, you've become the target for the new group...Jack must have told them about your whereabouts....actually, as per the information I've got, he is also stuck up in the city and is trying hard to leave the country!....so be careful and try to leave the city immediately!...I'm also leaving...All the best bro...Bye!", the person cut the call.

'So...my entry was a trap! Jack was behind it!', Rahul is stunned and sat down on the bed motionless for some time.

He came into the reality as there is knocking sound on the room door.

'Who's this?', Rahul is rattled as his tension is rising up again.

As the knocking sound is continued, Rahul stood up and opened the door. Three persons are standing across the door. He never saw them. They are suspiciously looking at him.

"Are you Rakesh?", the short man who came into the room asked in a hoarse voice.

His eyes are scanning Rahul from top to bottom. The other persons standing in front of the door also looking at him suspiciously. All are sturdy and rough. The alcohol smell coming from them engulfed the air in the room.

Rahul got some jerking shiver for a second.

'Are they from mafia?.... they must have tracked my movements! They're following me!?', Rahul thought for a while.

"No...I'm Arjun...what's the matter?", Rahul replied in a cool voice filled with confusion.

He had taken the room in the name, Arjun, coming from the neighbouring state on personal work.

"Where from you came?...how long you're staying here?", the short man asked in an interrogative tone.

"I've come from the Coastal state on personal work two days ago...I'll stay here for another two days ... Anyway, what's the matter?...who're you? And who's this Rakesh?", Rahul replied sternly looking into the eyes of the short man.

The short man stood there for a few seconds staring into Rahul's eyes.

"We're from police department...in search of a person called Rakesh...Okay...sorry for the trouble", he stepped out of the room.

Rahul stood there with a sigh of relief. All the three persons turned back and went downstairs. Rahul heard while they were going down that one of them telling the short man to make a call to Jack.

Rahul got panic! He recollected the conversation with the old colleague who warned him to leave the city immediately before they would find him.

'Yes...they're from mafia...Jack must've sent them to nab me!', Rahul clearly felt the shivering sensation all over the body.

Sweating started though the ceiling fan is running in full speed.

'What to do now? Luckily, they went away without much interrogation! If they contact Jack and ensure that I'm Rakesh, whom they're searching for...then...It would be risky to hang around here...better to change the location!' Rahul decided.

'Tomorrow Imran is arriving... I should find a safe place till I meet him...Better to inform him now itself and better to make a whatsapp call...that would be less risky', Rahul thought while packing his clothes into the bag.

He rang up Imran's number. It is not getting connected. He tried a few more times. No use. Rahul stopped that attempt and engaged in packing his luggage. Within five minutes he got ready. Slowly he came out of the room and looked around. The corridor is empty. He quickly went down to the reception. Within ten minutes, he vacated the room and came onto the road. He looked around cautiously. The mafia gang who had come to his room were not seen. He crossed the road and reached Omega hotel. The time is around five in the evening. The crowd is slowly increasing in the Tea section. Rahul took his cup and started sipping the tea looking around. He tried to be casual. None seemed suspicious.

'They must've left!', Rahul sighed in relief.

He came out and lit a cigarette standing at a corner of the road. The evening traffic is on the rise and the winter darkness already set in. Lights in the nearby commercial shops have turned on. Slowly it turned dark. He wanted to wait till it becomes complete dark so that he can move freely. After spending there for another half an hour, Rahul slowly moved onto the road and started to walk towards the nearby auto stand. He settled into an auto and told the driver about the destination. Suddenly, the short person who had interrogated him in the hotel room, came across and stopped the auto.

He straightly came to Rahul and asked him "Where're you going..Rakesh!", His voice is more hoarse now.

His eyes are sternly looking at him with an expression that you cannot escape from them! Rahul did not expect their sudden appearance. He has got panic but tried to calm down and appear cool.

"Who's Rakesh?...Why did you come again...I'm going out on urgent work...get aside", Rahul tried to be curtly.

"Get down you bastard!...you can't escape from us!", that person suddenly held Rahul's shirt collar tightly.

Rahul saw that the other two persons are approaching the Auto. Rahul suddenly pushed the short man onto the road and yelled at the auto driver to move fast. The driver who is also surprised at the sudden scuffle, has got normal and moved the auto immediately. The short man who fell onto the road got up and tried to chase the auto along with the other two persons. But the auto zoomed along the road and merged into the traffic. Rahul looked back while his heart is thumping. His shirt got wet with the running sweat. He saw two bikes are following him! They are four in total, two each on a bike. They are trying to catch the auto. But with the increased vehicular traffic, they are a few metres away from the auto. Rahul turned his head and looked forward. The road is getting narrower and soon would be left with less traffic as the driver is running the auto as per the address told him. Actually Rahul gave him a vague destination. He wanted to search for a safe resort after reaching the destination. As the bikes are still following the auto though a few metres away, Rahul turned panic again. He looked around. The Street is divided into many small lanes on both sides of the main road. He felt it would not be safe to move on in the auto. Because, they can reach him within a few minutes as they are riding rashly behind a few vehicles away from the auto.

"Turn into the right lane and stop!", Rahul told the auto driver.

The driver swiftly turned the auto into the right side lane and moved fast a few metres ahead and turned again into a left side small lane which is already in dark.

"Better get down Sir...hide somewhere before they come!", the driver told him breathing heavily.

He looked frightened. But tried to save him from the persons chasing behind. Rahul ran out of the auto pushing a few notes into the hand of the driver. He started to run along the dark by-lane without looking back. He turned right and left into a few more by-lanes of the slum residential locality. As it is a winter night, the small lanes looked desert with less movement of people. After running a few lanes, he stopped at a place where a compound wall appeared at the end of the lane. The street dogs lying on the sides of the lane got up and started barking at him. Rahul got panic. He thought that it would be better to climb over the compound wall before people came out of houses on hearing the barking sound of the street dogs. He looked at the compound wall. It looks old with cracks here and there. Beyond it, an old building is seen with scanty lighting and with big trees covering the building all over its premises. Rahul looked back. None was seen. He jumped over the compound wall. It was almost dark there. He could see the area around him owing to the scanty light coming from the front side of the building. Rahul stood there for a while and slowly looked over the wall just to ensure whether anyone saw him jumping over the wall. As none is seen, he slowly walked towards the front side of the building.

It is a two storied building in a dilapidated state. The compound wall gate is closed. There are no lights in the building. The light spread in the front side only because of the street lights located near the compound wall gate. He reached the compound wall gate and looked through it. Beyond the gate, every side is covered with internal roads of the residential locality except on the left side of the building which is seen full of big trees which looks like a small forest area. Rahul came back to the building. It has a spacious portico. He decided to stay there tonight as it would not be safer to move around at night time. The portico is filled with dried leaves. He cleaned a corner and sat down there. He looked in his mobile. It is around eleven. He felt hungry. Afternoon, he had a small and quick lunch. Since then, because of this chasing, he got tired. Rahul searched his bag and found that a water bottle is there. He drank some water. He slowly closed his eyes and soon turned into sleep.

****

"That means...Rahul is a trapped victim in this mafia!, isn't it?!", Inspector Vinay looked at Sheela sipping the coffee served by his wife Padma.

Both are sitting in the drawing room of his residence. Sheela nodded her head with a delighted look indicating that he finally got the point she has tried to present before him from all the possible angles for the last half an hour. She strived very hard showing him all the evidences from her laptop.

"Sheela!... have this sweets...my mother sent them!", Padma came with a plate full of sweets.

Vinay wondered how Sheela could manage to convince her to meet him at home. He was so surprised that Sheela came to his house without informing him in advance. By the time he reached home, both Padma and Sheela were seen sitting in the drawing room fully engaged in a chitchat emanating loud laughter. She directly contacted Padma and with her invitation only she had come here. When Padma phoned him that Sheela was coming home to talk to him a confidential matter of the important case they were dealing with, he was surprised and slightly got panic. Actually, by the time Padma phoned him, he was on the way to home.

Sheela was smart enough to know that he would soon reach home.

'Thank God!, Sheela really saved me!...Otherwise, It'd have been very difficult for me to convince Padma that this beautiful young girl is just a mere official colleague and they didn't have any other damned relations or affairs!", Vinay felt relieved.

"By the way, where is this Imran?, when would he be in our contact!?", Vinay asked.

He felt relaxed because, now he has got the clarity that Sheela has been fully engaged in locating the mafia core circle and has already made a very big exercise together with her team. The evidences she has shown are very vital. Just some more loose ends are needed to present the whole picture.

"I had to try very hard to find Imran's whereabouts Sir!....Luckily...he had arrived into the City from Mumbai last night only....As I said earlier, I had spoken to him in detail about all the matters related to Rahul...Already Rahul has been in contact with him.... Rahul is ready to confess his involvement in the drug racket...the matter is that once we can track Rahul's phone, we'll be able to reach him....actually he is being chased by the mafia...his life is at risk!", Sheela kept on telling him at a stretch as if she is in a hurry.

Vinay observed the concern in her voice.

"Okay Sir...I'm leaving...once our team got the track of Rahul's phone, we need a police party to reach him....In the meanwhile, I am going to meet Imran. Just now he sent a message of the meeting place", Sheela stood up looking into her mobile.

"Keep using that hired vehicle till completion of this operation", Vinay told her.

She nodded in consent and went into the kitchen to take leave from his wife too.

****

Rahul suddenly woke up and looked around. For a moment, he could not understand where he is sleeping. After few seconds, he realized that he fell asleep on the portico of the building and now suddenly woke up because of some sounds which alerted his mind. He looked around. Nothing seemed suspicious. He looked at his mobile. It is around two thirty. The residential locality around the building is silent except the squeaking sounds of insects. He took some water from the bottle. Then searched his bag and found the cigarette packet in the side packet. He lit a cigarette.

'I Should move from here before dawn so that I can reach a safe place suitable for meeting Imran....his phone seems out of network coverage...perhaps he may be on the way by train', Rahul thought.

Suddenly, he heard a thudding sound along with a bang on the backside of his head with a heavy object. He felt his head got numb for a few seconds. He could not understand what happened. But, quickly he sensed the danger realizing that somebody hit him hard with a stick from back side. He tried to stand up. Again there is the same thudding sound. But this time, as Rahul is bending down to get up, the blow of the stick like object touched strongly on his left shoulder. Rahul quickly rolled on the floor to escape from the banging. While rolling he looked around. He could see in the scanty lighting, four persons standing on a corner with sticks in their hands. Rahul realized that they finally traced him. Before he got up, two persons jumped on to him and started to beat him with hard sticks. Rahul came into full senses.

'Yes...they came to eliminate me!...I should escape from here!', Rahul confirmed the situation himself.

He kicked hard on the thighs of a person and pulled the leg of the second person with a hand. Both of them fell down losing balance. Rahul quickly got up like a spring. He jumped over them and ran towards the other two persons who already came towards him menacingly.

'I can't run from them so easily....better to face them', He thought quickly.

Both the persons raised sticks to bang on his head once again. Rahul did not give them chance this time. He quickly held the hand of one person firmly and pulled him aside while kicking the second person in the belly. He fell down on the side wall of the portico with his head hitting on the wall. He could not get up immediately. In the meanwhile, the other two persons who attacked Rahul first jumped onto him and held him firmly. Rahul tried to get rid of their hold. The third person, the short man, came forward and kicked hard in Rahul's stomach. Rahul felt that his stomach became flat with that blow. The short man started to pound him with strong punches on his face. Rahul felt blood flow from his nose and teeth.

"Kill the son of a bitch!", the short man ordered the fourth one who came forward and stabbed a knife into Rahul's stomach.

Rahul yelled loudly with pain. As he was damn tired and didn't eat anything since two days, and also he was on chase till now, his energies and strength started to get deteriorated. Moreover, these strong punches and stabbing wound made him weak. Rahul realized that they are going to finish him. He felt very angry for his plight.

'Why should I give up my life to these street sides goons? ... I should leave the place immediately', Rahul thought while kicking the person who stabbed him.

As he kicked him with such a force with his two legs, the person was thrown away beyond the portico like a dried piece of wood. He has not got up. By the force he used, the two persons holding him loosened their grip. But he tightly held their necks with his two hands and raised his legs and kicked the short man with his strength. The short man jumped a little in the air and was thrown towards the door of the building. On hitting the door strongly, he slid down to the floor and fell motionless. In the meanwhile, it took time for the remaining two persons to react and get released from his tight hold. Rahul took off his hands from their necks and gave a big punch on the face of one who yelled with pain and fell down on his knees. The last person tried to hold Rahul again. But, without giving him scope, Rahul turned towards him and started to give big blows on his face. The person fell backwards wall with a sound. Rahul swiftly, took up one of the sticks they brought and started to bang them on their heads. The short man sprang up and ran towards the main gate of the compound wall. Rahul ran behind him. He is in no mood to leave them conscious. He wanted to beat them like pulp. He reached him quickly and kicked him on his back while he was trying to climb up the metal gate. Suddenly, a vehicle stopped in front of the gate. Rahul recognized it as a police vehicle. For a couple of seconds, his mind did not work. While he is standing there motionless, four or five police persons in the civil dress, got down and started to climb over the gate.

"Stop there!, Don't' move!" one of them focused a torch light on his face.

He is holding a revolver in his hand.

Rahul quickly turned back and started to run towards left side of the building where it is complete dark and full of big trees beyond the compound wall. He climbed up the compound wall and jumped down into the woods. But, contrary to his expectation, there is no road or normal surface on that side. Beyond the compound wall, there is a slope full of bushes and rocks which leads into a pit. Rahul landed on a sloped rock and rolled down to the bottom of the pit where his head hit a rock. He fell unconscious.

****

CHAPTER FIFTEEN

Rahul slowly tried to open his eyes. But, he felt it is hard to raise his eye lids so easily. He has heard many voices from his sleep since a long time. Some voices seemed familiar. He realized that he is coming out of a deep sleep. Though he is trying to open his eyes, he is not able to open completely. The vision seemed blurred.

'Where am I? .... Who're talking continuously while I was sleeping?', he thought for a while.

'Anyhow, I should get up', he decided and tried to open his eyes again.

This time, his efforts succeeded. He could open his eyes completely. Everything looked bright and white around. The ceiling and the walls appeared white. He realized that he is lying on a bed. He looked around. A person was seen sitting on his bed side with a concerned look. Rahul looked at him for a few seconds and recognized him.

'It's Imran!...Oh! He has come for me! So everything will be alright!', Rahul felt happy but fell asleep again though he tried hard to be conscious.

"Rahul....Rahul...look at me *Yaar*!", Rahul heard Imran's voice.

Rahul tried to open his eyes again but he felt it is not so easy.

'Why couldn't I get up earlier? Why did I fell asleep again?', Rahul thought for a while.

Though still feeling sleepy, this time he realized that he woke up and fell asleep again just after seeing Imran sitting on his bed side. He has also realized that he was lying on a bed in a hospital. Slowly, he tried to recollect what happened while he was asleep.

'Yes...doctors, nurses and some more persons kept on talking...I could hear some unknown voices also along with Imran's voice and one more familiar female voice. Who's that?', His mind is trying to recollect.

While he was sleeping, he had also heard a female voice crying aloud so close to his ears. He tried to stir his head and body. He felt the body is lying like a log and numb.

"Rahul...Rahul", Imran is calling him slowly.

This time Rahul tried using his full strength and could open his eyes. He looked at Imran.

"Thank God!...came into life!", Imran was seen with delighted eyes.

Rahul looked at him for a few seconds. There's a lot of change in Imran's face and body. He looked like a grown up man. He has slightly grown up beard and mustaches. Now he is looking more handsome. Rahul looked around. A nurse is standing at a corner of the room searching for some medicines. It seemed a corporate hospital with all the facilities. He looked at himself. There are bandages around his hands and IV set is fixed to one hand. He is feeling slight pain somewhere around his head and stomach. He tried to move his hand. It moved slightly. He felt relieved. Suddenly, it struck to his mind.

'Yes...after the scuffle and fight with the mafia goons and police chase, I had jumped over the compound wall and fell into a deep pit...then, how did I come into this hospital?...who admitted me here?...If it's police, then I should have been in a government hospital!...Certainly,

Imran must have reached there and found me there in the pit!', Rahul's thoughts are going on guessing the events happened before his present condition in this hospital bed.

He again looked at Imran. He is not there. He is standing at the door and talking to someone in his mobile. The nurse came to him. She raised and adjusted the bed to make him in a slightly elevated position upto his waist.

"Open your mouth please...you have to swallow this pill", she asked with a smiling face.

Imran came back to him. He looked at him with a satisfaction in his eyes.

"How do you feel Rahul?", Imran's voice sounded so concerned.

"Okay...I feel okay...but some slight pain somewhere...I don't know where...when did you come?...How I came here?", Rahul felt happy that though feeble, he is able to speak and audible to himself too.

"Oh God!...so much talking...thank God...Really God saved you!...after so much blood lost and with multiple injuries you have been unconscious for the last three days you know?", Imran is going on speaking in a flow because his joy has no bounds that Rahul is now able to recognize him and also speaking properly.

"Three days?...who admitted me here?...tell me Imran!", Rahul asked him on hearing that he was unconscious for three days.

"Yes Yaar!...You have undergone a surgery too...so many stiches...so much blood was sent into your body...you've been on saline since you were brought here by the police party who were searching for you...Anyway, by God's grace, we have got you back from the clutches of death...thank God!". Imran turned emotional once again.

'Oh! I got a surgery too!', Rahul surprised.

Suddenly, he recollected that he was stabbed by one of the goons. But it puzzled him why police had admitted him in this high end corporate hospital. Though he asked Imran twice since he woke up, he has not given any clarity on that.

"Nurse already told me to give you liquid food first...first drink this juice Rahul...open your mouth", Imran come with a glass of juice and put it near his mouth.

Rahul slowly sipped the juice. He felt the juice is tasty as he felt hungry because he has been living on saline for the last three days. While he is sipping the juice, suddenly the door opened. He saw a doctor in white dress with a stethoscope around his neck came along with two police officers and one young lady in jeans. On seeing the police, Rahul got stiffened. The young lady rushed to him. He looked at her. He felt he had seen her earlier.

"Rahul!...How do you feel now!?", She asked him with a broad smile on her face.

Rahul stared at her. Suddenly, he recognized her. She is Sheela.

'How Sheela came here?...that too along with police!?', his mind got puzzled.

He looked at her with a confused mind. On seeing them, Imran also got up and looked at them with a smile as if he is waiting for them.

"He is okay now...all the vitals are working well...he can recover fully within ten days", the Doctor told the police after examining him and on seeing the case sheet.

"You're lucky Rahul!...if Sheela hadn't traced your exact location, your life would've been in danger!...we're happy that you're alright now!", One of the police Officer told him.

Rahul did not speak anything. He looked at his name badge.

'Vinay Kumar, Inspector of Police', Rahul could read the letters.

"Okay Sheela!...it's upto you...let him take rest tonight.....we'll start our work tomorrow morning!", Inspector turned towards Sheela and looked at Rahul and said, "Okay Rahul!. We'll meet again", the police officer left the room along with the doctor.

Rahul looked at Sheela. She is looking at him. She looked into his eyes. He noticed a slight film of tears in her eyes. He saw a lot of change in her face, dress and hair style.

"Thanks Sheela!", Rahul said in a low voice looking at her, though he could not understand how she located him.

She settled on the stool beside his bed. His left hand is already in her hands. She's already caressing his hand.

"Oh! You know saying thanks to others! Great change!", Sheela said in a teasing voice with a mischievous look into his eyes.

"Isn't it Imran?!", she looked at Imran.

"Yes!", Imran endorsed nodding his head vigorously.

Both appeared in a cheerful mood. Rahul couldn't understand what's going on... how Sheela located him, how Imran joined them,...how police are so positive towards him.....and how he was admitted in a corporate hospital. Questions are swirling in his mind without finding replies to any of them.

Sheela looked into his eyes again. She understood that he is in a confused state of mind over the incidents happened for the last few days.

"Don't think too much Rahul! Be relaxed!...soon we'll get rid of all these problems!...Okay?", Sheela told him in a low and soothing voice looking into his eyes.

Though he has not got any reply, Rahul felt relieved. He never had such experience of the way she talked to him so intimately, so kindly and soothingly. But, he liked it. Her presence and speech is giving him strong assurance that he would be out of this mess soon. He tried to nod his head. While he is going to say thanks again, Sheela stood up as her mobile started ringing. She was engaged in talking over phone at a corner of the room. After a minute, she came back to him.

"Rahul...I have to move on now as my colleagues are calling....take rest...Imran!...stay for the night....doctor told that he can start eating normal food from tomorrow morning....I'll bring breakfast Okay..?" Sheela spoke to both of them at a stretch and left the room in a hurry.

Imran followed her upto the door and came back.

"What's the time now?", Rahul asked him.

"It's nine in the night...now take some more juice...tomorrow morning you can eat the breakfast Sheela would bring...Okay?" Imran again put a full glass of orange juice near his lips.

Rahul slowly started to sip the juice. After Rahul finished the juice, Imran wiped his lips and started to tell what happened.

"Really, we have to be thankful to Sheela!...without her, our story in this case, would have been different Rahul!...Sheela is now working in police department you know?....She is assisting them in solving big cases...she is having a team....they work on laptops and technology...you know?...she said...they can solve cyber-crime cases also...she's been working on this drug mafia case for several months....and you know one thing?... she saw your footage where you're escaping from police raid on a pub...she recognized you even seeing from back!" Imran started to unfold the things happened without his knowledge.

Rahul is listening with the rising surprise over the new and unimagined things about Sheela.

"Sheela is working in police department?...I have never expected about her entering this field!", Rahul expressed his surprise looking at Imran.

Now he has come into full consciousness. Since the consolation got from the words of doctor and the way the police officer and Sheela talked and now the things Imran telling- all made him feeling that he has got into a comfort zone.

"Yes Rahul!...She must have studied higher technical courses and got trained....After you vacated your room without telling her...she had tried a lot to find your whereabouts....but the poor girl kept on searching for you without knowing that you were fallen prey into this field...she said until she recognized you in that pub footage...she did not know about me too...but suddenly she recollected that see had seen me along with you in a couple of times....once she had seen us at our shop in the old city...so she went there to find me...And she got my mobile number from Mastan Bhai...Once she got that...she came into contact with me....Actually, by the time she contacted me, you're already in touch with me and I was also about to start to reach here by train....she said she is eagerly waiting for me...through me she got your mobile number also....she told me not to call you...because your call list already under the surveillance of mafia...I would also be in danger...that's why I didn't lift your calls...But, she started to track your location and alerted the police...they correctly located you...by that time you have already finished the fight with those buggers...police arrested all of them...before they tried to run away from the scene...Police saw you climbing down the wall and falling into a pit....you condition was so critical...you know? multiple injuries on hands!...on legs...back of your head and more particularly...a deep stab in your stomach...you fell unconscious as you lost a lot blood....once police took out you from the pit...Sheela came into contact with them...it was her decision to admit you in this hospital...it's confidential...you know?....mafia should not know your whereabouts....once you're brought, doctors had done a surgery for your stabbing wound...five stiches you know?....but thank God!...you have been recovering well...and by the way...once you're brought here, Sheela informed me to come to this hospital as she was also on the way....We both reached at the same time...Once seen you on the bed unconscious and with so many wounds, she fell on you and sobbed a lot.... After the surgery, she sent me to take rest and herself stayed here for two nights!.. Such a kind girl she is!...Really without her, I couldn't have found your whereabouts and couldn't have saved you!...I'm saying the truth Yaar!....she redeemed herself from what she owed to you for that what you did to her when she was in distress...once you saved her... now she reciprocated...really great!.. Who knows what happens at what time!....Really God is great!", Imran went into spiritual mode for a while.

'Yes...I owed her for saving my life!', Rahul thought.

His mind filled with a feel of gratitude while thinking about the way she had saved him from the position he was struggled in a few days ago and now on this bed in police protection. While he is still thinking deeply about the course of action, a junior nurse came with a flask.

"Please give him the milk...Sheela madam sent this...let him take rest for now...tomorrow morning...he would be given a mouth wash...then you can start giving him breakfast and normal diet" She told Imran putting the flask on the table and left.

Imran filled a cup of hot milk and gave it to Rahul. While sipping the hot milk he felt his energies got rejuvenated.

"Yaar....there's a cafeteria downstairs...I'll come back after having some light dinner...close your eyes and go to sleep...okay!" Imran wiped Rahul's lips with a napkin. Rahul nodded like a child and closed his eyes. Slowly he fell into deep sleep.

****

"Good morning Rahul!", Rahul raised his head on hearing the voice.

It's a new voice. A young girl in jeans is standing in front of him. He has never seen her. Next to her, one young man also in jeans is standing and looking at him with a cheerful face. Rahul looked at them with confusion filled eyes.

"Yes. I can understand your confusion....you don't know who we're!... I'm Vineeta and He's Pradeep!...we're team mates of Sheela...hope now you got it!", the young girl told without waiting for a second for his response or reaction.

Rahul looked at her. She is a little younger to Sheela. But unlike her, she is bubbly. Whenever she talks, she raises her head and eyes in a rhythmic way and her pony tail also moves in the same direction.

"Hi. Rahul!" the young man also wished him with gentle smile. He is wearing glasses and carrying a laptop bag. He looks gentle and seems a man of less words.

Rahul smiled at them. It's seven in the morning. Imran woke up him by six itself. Nurse came and gave him mouth wash and slight body wash. Clothes were also changed. Imran already fed him with the breakfast sent by Sheela. The homemade hot Idli Sambar combo got a new life to the taste buds of his tongue. Rahul enjoyed it and after that got a cup of coffee.

As he felt refreshed and waiting for the nurse to give him morning dose of medicines, these two persons came in as if they were waiting outside till he finished the breakfast.

Imran smiled at them and offered them small chairs brought from a corner of the room.

'So they're the people whom Sheela's working with!', Rahul thought looking at them.

'They have come so early in the morning means now I should tell them about drug mafia!', Rahul is thinking.

"See Rahul...since you've been recovering well and doctors assured that you're out of danger and get well soon, we can start our job, isn't it?", Pradeep paused his introduction of the topic he is going to take up.

"Yes Sir! Rahul is ready to cooperate with you people...Actually, he was attacked by the goons when he was coming to meet and tell the police about how he was trapped in this mafia!", Imran intervened before Rahul could respond.

"That's good...soon Sheela will join us. We can start to collect all the required information from you", Vineeta said looking at both Rahul and Imran.

Just when he is nodding his head in consent, Sheela entered the room along with Inspector Vinay and two more new persons who came with some big bags. Vinay is in plain clothes. The other two persons appear as police in plain clothes.

On seeing them, both Pradeep and Vineeta stood up attentively. Two more persons came in with half a dozen plastic chairs and arranged them around Rahul's bed.

Sheela looked at Rahul. As he appeared active, fully conscious and active with a refreshed looks, Sheela smiled at him satisfactorily.

"How're you Rahul?, how do you feel now?", Inspector Vinay asked him.

"I'm fine Sir", Rahul replied with a clear voice.

"Thanks! The breakfast was good...I've taken food first time after a gap of a week...That's why I feel strong now" Rahul said to Sheela with a thankful tone.

"You'll get lunch and dinner too....be ready for getting more and more strong!" Sheela responded with a graceful smile.

"Rahul.. Our team will start to ask you all that you know about the mafia", Inspector Vinay told smoothly with a hidden authority in his tone.

Rahul nodded his head.

"Sheela, I have to move now...I have to accompany ACP to meet Commissioner Sir by ten thirty...Once you finished your job in whatever way you can do...give me a ring...I'll come back to station...Okay!" Inspector Vinay got up looking at Sheela.

As the Inspector left the room, Sheela dragged her chair close to Rahul.

"Rahul...please tell me whatever you know about the drug mafia.... How you were trapped into it ...when you first met Jack...how long you worked....the places and persons you have supplied the stuff...all that...everything without hiding or forgetting...we need everything...see.... you have been brought here very confidentially...police are on patrol around the hospital premises and inside hospital too in plain clothes...The police department has taken all the precautions without giving any scope for the mafia to smell about your presence here...the goons who attacked you and got beaten by you were all arrested and in police custody now...they were being interrogated... we gathered very little information from them...because they're engaged just to finish you... they didn't have any direct connection with drug supply...Once I met Imran, I got your mobile number tracked...Now our team already started examining all the numbers in contact with you for the last one year...Vinnie and Pradeep will be on that job...We've traced your apartment too...we examined everything there...we did not get anything useful there...More importantly...I want to know more about this notorious international drug peddler...Jack...till now the Department is not having any clear photograph of the person...now our team members will draw his picture with your help...Okay?" Sheela stopped for a few seconds as if to take breath after talking at a stretch.

While Sheela nodded her head looking at the two persons who came with a big bag, they opened their bags and took out pads, a lap top and other drawing material. In the meanwhile, two police persons came in and served tea for all.

Rahul closed his eyes for a few seconds and sighed in relief. It is very surprising for him to see a new person in Sheela. The way she is moving, talking, looking and everything of her is so professional and official. She looks quite different from what he saw a year ago before he had left that old roof top room.

For the next five to six hours, Sheela has kept on asking him of all the information related to his job and connections. Her team mates Vineeta and Pradeep asked him about each phone number he talked to. In between, the forensic artists who came with drawing material showed different photos to Rahul and on his suggestions, they started to draw the sketch of Jack. Rahul wondered how Jack escaped so long without showing his face to police all these years...Here and there Sheela questioned Imran too. While Rahul was telling about each and every incident...both Imran and Sheela looked at him surprisingly how a person known to them involved in this field so deeply. Rahul told her about how he got into this field...how he first met Jack...how he was offered a job in this field...how he was engaged himself in receiving, stocking, distributing, selling the stuff and remitting the amount collected. He told about the places, areas he visited, the persons he worked with, the clients whom he supplied the drugs. He told of the different forms in which the drug was received and disposed to the end customers. He told about the residential areas, schools, colleges, hotels, pubs to which the stuff was supplied. He told her how he got his earnings or commission while remitting the collected cash. She also inquired about the sequence of events starting from when he was caught in CCTV footage at the backside of the pub to the fight with the mafia goons and fell into pit with wounds at the old bungalow. Rahul has kept on answering all the questions raised by Sheela and her team mates. The artists drew Jack's face changing the features as per the suggestions of Rahul. Finally they could arrive at the face which Rahul endorsed almost similar to that of Jack. He felt wondered how the technology could be utilized in crime investigation. Once, Jack's figure has been achieved, the artists left the room with their material. Sheela asked them to send her the computerized graphic images of Jack once got ready at the lab. Then Sheela has checked with her team mates that they have noted down all the important points they could secure from Rahul. Once satisfied that almost everything is covered, they all got up with satisfaction.

"Rahul it's already two thirty...sorry we forgot about your lunch! It's already arrived...please have it and take rest" Sheela told in a low voice looking at Rahul and turning towards Imran, she asked "would you need any break tonight, Imran?"

"No...Sheela!...I'll stay here only....Moreover, Rahul is conscious now....he needs my company", Imran replied hurriedly.

He is calling her by name as she strongly insisted not to call her, 'Madam'.

"Good...Okay Rahul...Bye!", Sheela left the room together with her team.

As soon as she left, Imran opened the lunch carrier. He is very hungry. It is new thing for him to see such a prolonged investigation starting from the morning to beyond lunch session. So is the case with Rahul. Both of them seemed tired of facing the continuous questionnaire and drawing sketches of Jack.

"Wow!, It's chicken curry Yaar!....let's have...it's already too late.", Imran exclaimed with a delighted face while opening the carrier.

For the last four days, he has not taken proper food because of Rahul's condition. Imran served the food to Rahul in a plate. Now Rahul is able to eat himself because of the adjustable bed and the dining plank.

"Really we must be thankful to Sheela! She's handling the situation very well", Rahul said while enjoying the food.

"Yes!", Imran chorused chewing a chicken piece.

"If everything goes well and the police come out successful in busting the mafia, it would give me a lot of satisfaction! I don't bother how many years I would be in jail", Rahul stated thoughtfully.

"Since you're cooperating the investigation, I think you'll be out of jail within a year....Sheela would see that I hope!", Imran is still in the mood of savoring the food.

"If it's one year, I would be lucky! By the way, what about your marriage?" Rahul asked him suddenly.

"Oh!...you're thinking of my marriage!...don't forget the position we're in!...Anyway...still we are having enough time....it would take place whenever I say okay...they don't know that I'm in the city...you know?!", Imran laughed.

They finished lunch hurriedly. While they are taking rest, nurse came and got checked his BP and temperature. She declared that everything normal and he is recovering well.

****

Rahul has recovered well within next five days with regular food, medicines and health care. His surgical wounds also heeled quickly. Now he is able to sit and walk in the room. He is feeling well. Imran continued staying there because Sheela told him not to move outside as they are under strict surveillance. They have accustomed to the daily routine. Sheela is coming every morning with breakfast and enquiring about his condition. It has been a regular routine for Rahul to wait for her arrival. From the next day of investigation, she's been coming in chudidar in which Rahul used to see her when he was at the roof top room. She's looking graceful. Imran noticed that she's taking extra care in her make up.

On the sixth day morning, Sheela came with a broad smile on her face.

"Good news for us! Jack's caught! ", Sheela exclaimed like a kid.

Both Rahul and Imran looked at her with amused faces.

"He was hiding in a slum area of the old city...it's a great success for the department!...our team worked very hard in tracking him...he's been changing his mobile SIMs very frequently....for the last four days two or three times, he escaped narrowly....but his picture has helped us a lot...finally...last night we're able to zeroed in on his location...in the early hours, special police parties surrounded his hide out and nabbed him safely and now he's being interrogated at a secret place!", Sheela concluded sipping the tea served by Imran.

Rahul felt relieved.

'Nabbing of Jack is the crucial thing...with his interrogation, the core mafia would come out', Rahul thought.

"What a news Sheela! Congrats to you and your team!...Really a great work done by you!...God bless you!", Imran told as his joy has found no bounds on hearing the news.

"By the way, Just now I've talked to the doctors...your stiches would be removed tomorrow morning and you'll be discharged tomorrow itself!", Sheela told looking at Rahul with delighted eyes.

"Thanks Sheela!", Rahul looked at her with wet eyes.

His voice faltered with sudden increase of hoarseness in his throat. She touched his hand looking at him surprisingly.

'There's been a lot of change in his looks and expressions now days...this dumb log can now be able to show emotions too!', She thought.

For a while, she could not speak anything. But she came back to normalcy quickly.

"And one more thing...your rented flat at the posh gated community is still in seize...so you can't go there...and it's not safe for you to stay outside too... the department arranged accommodation for you at the Police guest house!...both of you should stay there for a few more days...Okay?", Sheela declared the next course of action.

Both Rahul and Imran nodded in consent like school kids.

****

CHAPTER SIXTEEN

"Okay Imran! I'll bring the flowers too...Already I've collected your dress from Mastan Bhai ...I'll be there within an hour...I'm in traffic...after the passengers got down, I'll start!. Right?", Rahul cut the call and started his brand new cab.

He switched on the FM radio and adjusted the AC as asked by the passengers. The car is moving so smoothly. He never drove such a brand new top end model when he had worked as cab driver. Within half an hour, he reached the destination. The passengers got down paying the money over phone pay.

'Today the earnings are so surprising. Though I've been busy with wedding works of Imran since the morning ...I could earn three thousands!. That's great!', Rahul felt satisfied.

Then he drove straightly for a five kilometres without stopping anywhere till the wanted destination arrived. It's part of old city. He parked the car in a small lane and walked back to the main street and went into the nearest Irani restaurant. He ordered for a cup of tea. While sipping the tea, he casually observed around him. The hotel is full with the evening crowd. Slowly he opened the whatsapp account in his mobile and checked the photograph sent by Pradeep. Then he confirmed that it got matched with the person in green colour T-shirt sitting at a corner table and talking over phone for the last five minutes. Rahul has been keeping an eye on this person for the last two days. Now he is seen alone. He was involved in a ghastly murder cum robbery took place in the outskirts of the city a week ago. Police have been searching for him. Rahul sent a message to Pradeep and slowly came out of the restaurant. He stood near the adjacent pan shop and lit a cigarette. After a few minutes, the person in green colour T-shirt came out. Rahul crushed the cigarette butt under his shoe and started to follow him. The person immediately turned into a small lane. Rahul entered the lane but could not find the person. He suddenly disappeared. Rahul kept on going along the small lane which is divided into many narrowed sub-lanes on both sides. He slowly entered into a sub-lane which is dark with very little lighting. Suddenly, he looked back. The person in green colour T-shirt pounced on him with a knife in his hand. He is looking at Rahul menacingly. Rahul carefully caught hold of his hand and punched strongly on his face. The person yelled in pain. Rahul kicked him on his belly. He fell on the ground and tried to get up. Rahul kicked again on his head. He yelled with pain. Rahul swirled his hand forcibly and as he is yelling in pain, he took the knife from his hand. After throwing away the knife, Rahul pulled him up holding the collar of his T-shirt and banged his head to the wall of a house. He lost consciousness. Rahul dragged him out of the sub-lane. He lit a cigarette and waited for the arrival of police. A few minutes later, three constables came there. After handing over him to them, Rahul came out of the lane as if nothing happened and walked towards the place where he parked his cab.

Rahul looked at the time. It's five thirty in the evening. He drove the cab a kilometer and stopped near a tea shop where a passenger stopped his cab. As the passenger got into the cab, Rahul started the car. After a minute, it turned into a small lane where the passenger got down taking the plastic cover kept in the back seat. Once he got down, Rahul waited there for a few minutes. The passenger is a police constable for whom Rahul kept the cover to get collected.

As the delivery job is also over, Rahul started towards the function hall where Imran is staying in the adjacent hotel. Tomorrow morning Imran's wedding is going to take place.

'Time has galloping indeed!', Rahul thought.

His mind went back.

Three months have quickly passed since he discharged from the hospital fully recovered. He took a single bed room flat at a new residential locality and shifted into it vacating his rented flat in the gated community. He still remember the sequence of the incidents took place since the day Jack was caught. Jack revealed everything in the interrogation. The facts he told exposed many skeletons in the cupboard. Since the drug mafia has become a national threat, the central government took it very seriously. The mafia was proved as a big and powerful circle. The core of the drug mafia consisted of political leaders and business tycoons of the country. Seven political big shots were involved in the mafia including a minister of central government, three ministers of state government and one Member of Parliament of the Opposition. As the issue became so big, the national level investigation agencies also jumped into action. It took one and half a month to complete the process of covering all the culprits into the charge sheet. Almost all the core mafia was arrested.

Rahul bewildered by the hugeness of the mafia network. Even certain bad elements in the some central government departments also worked as helping sources for smooth transshipment of stuff in and out of the country.

Rahul could not forget the day on which he was brought to the office of the City Commissioner of Police. It was a secret meeting. He was brought from the backside of the building.

"I congratulate you and your team Sheela! You don't know what a great job you have done!", the Commissioner greeted Sheela.

Inspector Vinay accompanied him along with Sheela and her team. Three DCPs and one ACP were sitting in the Commissioner's Chamber.

"So, he is Mr. Rahul!", Commissioner asked Inspector Vinay looking at Rahul interestingly.

Rahul just wished him and couldn't say anything.

Vinay briefed the Commissioner in a low voice.

"Well young man, you played a key role in this case. Because of your cooperation, the bravery you had shown in fighting back and getting arrested the mafia goons and particularly, your inputs in catching Jack...Good!. You too deserve credit in this case!" Commissioner stated with a typical official tone.

Rahul blushed and murmured something in reciprocation.

"My staff told me very positive about you. Now, the Good news is that you are kept out of the case treating you as one of the top confidential informers. You will be provided with some job too if you're interested. Now tell me, would you like to assist the department as reliable informer? What do you say?, What Sheela!, Are you happy now?", Commissioner looked at both Sheela and Rahul.

Rahul could not believe his ears. He didn't expect this. Till then he was thinking that he would be sentenced with lesser jail term of about one or two years and thereafter, he would be free and he would find a job for his survival.

'But now they declared me as a free bird and that too with a job and also an additional employment!', Rahul wondered what's going on. He looked at Sheela. She gestured with her eyes to accept the offer.

"Thank you Sir, I will do whatever job is given Sir", Rahul replied in humble low voice.

Thereafter, things moved so quickly within a week. On the recommendation of Inspector Vinay, Rahul got a subsidized vehicle loan. Now he is the owner cum driver of his brand new cab. The day when he got delivery of the car from the showroom, Sheela jumped in joy just like a kid. As an informer to the department, every day, Rahul has to take daily assignments or tasks through Sheela's team. Within a month he has become busy in attending the tasks assigned to him. His daily routine includes tracking the movements of vehicles, keeping surveillance on individuals or delivery of confidential documents or articles to different places or stations of the police department.

Since Imran is interested to come back to city as he is going to marry a girl in the city itself, Sheela has arranged subsidized loan for Imran too with the help of the department, He opened a tailoring shop in the City. Inspector Vinay and Sheela jointly cut the ribbon inaugurating the shop a month ago. His fiancée is also very much eager to work in the shop. Imran is so happy now.

Sheela and her team have become very busy now. Her position has been elevated. She's been assigned with crucial cases including special cases recommended by national level agencies.

'It's very difficult to talk to Sheela now a days!', Rahul thought while parking the car in front of the hotel.

He got down taking the zipped cover in which the Imran's suit is packed. By the time he reached the hotel room, a few people had already gathered and were chatting with Imran. Being orphan like him, Imran too is not having close relatives.

The persons are his old friends and a few distant relatives gathered in his room to get ready him as bride groom. A couple of friends who are working along with him in Mumbai also came to attend his wedding. Rahul bought a gold ring for Imran as wedding gift. Imran felt very happy and cried holding Rahul when he showed him the gift.

"We got good days Yaar!...I'm very happy that your life has changed", Imran turned emotional hugging Rahul.

"It's all because of you Imran", Rahul smiled.

'Now a days this time of reciprocation from Rahul is very new and is coming out so spontaneously', Imran felt.

The gatherings, the hustled atmosphere, the arrangements going on and the ensuing wedding function made Rahul excited and joyous.

'Yes!, all this is new to me' Rahul thought watching the gathering.

He has also actively engaged in contacting bride's family members along with Imran's old master, Mastan. His frequent conversations with them over the ongoing arrangements made him more nearer to them because of his humble and responsive attitude. In fact, Imran's fiancée, Nazriya is showing a lot of interest in contacting Rahul. She is not leaving any occasion in chatting with Rahul as he is the only known close friend of Imran. She came to know everything about him, about their friendship, about how they grown up together, how Rahul saved his life. Imran told her everything about him except his involvement in the drug case.

Now also he got a call from Nazriya about to send the pics of Imran's suit. While he is busy in taking a couple of snaps and sending the pics to Nazriya, his mobile started ringing. He looked at the screen. It's from Sheela!

"Hello Sheela!", Rahul responded in a low voice wondering why she is calling now.

As per the information he got, she must be in New Delhi and should return by tomorrow early morning flight and he has to pick up her at the Airport. Sheela is silent. After a few seconds, Rahul got confused why she is not talking though he lifted her call.

"Hello Sheela!", he again responded increasing his voice.

"Not bad...you're able to lift the call immediately and can also wait to listen", She responded with a low and steady voice.

Rahul surprised by the sternness in her voice.

'What's the matter, What went wrong?', Rahul got frightened with her words.

"What's there Sheela...I would always lift the call...by the way...when you are starting? I'll be waiting for you to pick up at the Airport", Rahul maintained low voice.

Again Sheela maintained silence for a few seconds and responded.

"I've already reached home... the work's been completed in New Delhi and that's why I could start by the afternoon flight...I hoped you would call me and come to the Airport to pick up me", Sheela told with less sternness in her voice.

Rahul got frightened more. He chided himself.

"Sorry Sheela!..I should have made a call...I was thinking that you would start by early morning flight...and that's why I thought it would be better to call you later...Sorry for the trouble!", Rahul wondered how best he is trying to pacify her.

"It's okay!. I already talked to Imran this afternoon...He said that you're fully busy with other works....that's why I didn't call you", Sheela told slowly.

Rahul felt relieved of the fear as he could hear the normal sweetness in her voice.

"Morning I would come to the function straight from home....Don't come for picking up me...I'm coming with Vinay Sir's family....Pradeep and Vinnie will join there...Okay!", Sheela explained in her usual tone and cut the call.

****

By the dawn of next day, the real festive mood of the ceremony began. Rahul could not sleep over the night. Though he was busy in extending his help, all the wedding related formalities have been completed with the active participation of bride's parents and relatives. As the function hall is meant for Islamic wedding ceremonies, all the arrangements went on well with the help of the *Imam* of the local Mosque under whose guidance the Nikah is going to take place. Rahul stayed there along with Imran chitchatting over the future of both. Then they started to get ready. Rahul changed into a traditional dress stitched by Imran himself. He never wore such a dress. He looked new to himself.

As said, Sheela arrived by sharp nine along with her team and Inspector Vinay's family. Both Sheela and Rahul looked at each other for a while. Rahul found an appreciation in her looks over his attire. He blushed and smiled diverting his eyes on her. Sheela came in a light green color silk saree. She looked gorgeous. Rahul never saw her in a saree. The well plaited hair into a long braid adorned with a small rose and a bunch of jasmine flowers with a matching green color sticker on her forehead gave her the complete traditional look. The light make up stood her as an additional attraction in the function. Though Rahul·tried a lot to resist looking at her frequently, he could not turn his eyes on her. On observing his plight, Sheela went into bride's room along with other female folk.

It took one full hour to complete the Nikah and after that Walima has begun. Both Nazriya and Imran looked as made for each other with the traditional wedding attire. Nazriya's big eyes looked more attractive with the neatly drawn black eyeliner. The Mehendi filled hands with a lot of bangles enhanced the beauty of the bride. Rahul wondered when he found that his eyes got wet on seeing both of them. He felt an undefined emotion ejecting out from inside. His thoughts went back to the days of their teenage where they struggled hard for mere survival. He got down from the wedding dais and stood near main gate of the function hall for a while.

While the photo session started with the newly wedded couple, Imran called Rahul to come over onto the dais. He wiped his face with a kerchief and went on the dais. At the same time, Sheela came onto the dais along with her group wishing the couple with a beautiful flowers bouquet and a big gift packet.

"Thank you Sheela for gracing the occasion!" Imran looked emotional.

"I'm very happy to see you becoming a family man. My best wishes for both of you... Wish you a happy married life!", Sheela wished the couple.

The sweetness in her voice while wishing them mesmerized Rahul. He kept on looking her with an awe filled eyes.

"It's only because of you Sheela....only because of you, Rahul and I have begun a new life!....I'm thankful for that for my entire life...particularly for Rahul....You have changed his life...the future is in your hands Sheela!...please don't forget that!", Imran turned emotional.

Rahul felt embarrassed to listen Imran talking to Sheela so emotionally about him.

"I've not found much change in your friend...tell that dumb log to think about his future!", Sheela responded with a quick glance at Rahul.

Her voice sounded a slight sarcastic blame on him. Rahul got puzzled with her looks and words.

"Please don't blame him Sheela...he's been like that since childhood....it takes a lot of effort to make him a normal person...only you can do that Sheela!..I am waiting for the big occasion of seeing him a family man...I will wait for that to happen", Imran turned more emotional holding her hands.

Rahul stood dumb without knowing how to respond or react over the conversation going on in his presence. Sheela looked at him for a while and went down along with Vineeta who accompanied her.

"What Yaar? Don't waste time...this is the right occasion...open your mind before her...first go and help her at meals! they all are going dining hall!", Imran ordered Rahul.

Rahul nodded his head and quickly went to dining section. He waited there for Sheela group. Once he saw them, he started to serve them with the Biryani filled plates. Sheela took the plate from him and went to a corner where already Inspector Vinay, his family and Sheela's team members are eating. Rahul stayed there till they finished eating. After they finished main course, Rahul came with an ice cream cup. Sheela took it with a glance at him.

“How long you stand here? go and take meals...you look tired with the wedding works”, Sheela told him with a low voice.

She is looking directly into his eyes while tasting the ice cream.

“I’ll have later”, Rahul murmured nodding his head like a kid.

“Didn’t you hear what Imran said? Are you not interested in becoming a family man?” Sheela’s voice sounded in official tone mixed with a hidden teasing.

Rahul tried to avoid her probing looks. He got frightened and bowed his head without saying anything. The situation is becoming an embarrassment again. Sheela looked at him for a while.

“First you try to learn how to respond if someone is saying something”, Sheela’s voice turned soft.

Rahul looked at her. Her eyes are probing and still waiting for some answer.

“Sheela...What can I say! Really I don’t know what to say...I can listen whatever you say...that’s all!”, Rahul said in a meek voice.

“Is it?,” Sheela responded quickly.

Rahul looked at her and bowed his head again.

“Take this” Sheela handed over him a plastic bag.

“What’s this?” Rahul looked at her while taking the bag from her.

“It’s a new shirt...light sky blue color...you look good in that....come home wearing this tomorrow morning at ten....Dad wants to see you and talk to you...try to be normal and impress both my mom and dad....they want their would be son in law is not only looking handsome but also a normal man so that he would become a nice family man... Okay?” Sheela told him and quickly turned back and went away from there making fast strides that made her braid dancing in a rhythmic way on her back.

Rahul got stunned with what she said. He kept on looking at her till she disappeared beyond the entrance.

****

Rahul woke up startled by the mobile alarm sound. It is six thirty in the morning. Till then he was in deep sleep. He opened eyes and looked at the roof for a while just to find where he is lying. It took him a few seconds to confirm that he is lying on his bed. He returned to his room at around one thirty last night after completing all the assigned tasks of the wedding function till midnight. The traffic was still at higher side as the year ending celebrations were going on every corner of the city. It took him one and a half hours to reach his flat. As he was fully tired due to lack of proper sleep for the last two days, he fell asleep as soon as lying on the bed. Now he is recollecting the course of events took place at the wedding ceremony one by one in a sequence. His thoughts hovered around the duration of Sheela's arrival in a gorgeous attire with graceful looks and her exit with a finishing touch.

'Did Sheela mean what she had said?...Does she like me?...She loves me?'...Do I deserve it", Rahul wondered.

Last night while returning from the function hall, Rahul told Imran about what she had said to him. Imran hugged him tightly with a broad smile on his face.

"This is what I wanted for you Yaar!...go home and take rest...Tomorrow I should listen the great news from you!...because it's new year's day and more importantly your birthday!....Happy birthday in advance Yaar!", Imran wished him and hurried him.

Though Rahul tried to tell him something, Imran was not in a mood to listen. Forced by him, he had to leave the venue.

'Yes....if Imran says so it must be true!...She must be in love with me...I deserve it!...yes...I'm a lovable person!....a girl told me that she was ready to enter into my life!', Rahul felt that this confirmation is giving him immense satisfaction of achieving something which he could not have dreamt of.

An undefined feeling started swirling inside him which made his heart thumping with increased beat.

Suddenly, his thoughts went back to his childhood and getting oscillated there searching for memories of connecting or dealing with women. He did not know how would be his mother's love and affection. He was brought up by his uncle for a few years but no female had come so close to him in place of his mother till he was in his village. Though he used to deal with young girls, women folk as part of his livelihood when his life started in the city, none had come close to him and he too never tried to get close to any girl. All his time was spent on earning something for survival. In teenage, he strictly followed the habit of keeping himself away from the adolescent infatuations whenever he come across any good looking girl. He used to tell himself that he did not deserve such costly affairs because he looked it that way. Even after grown into a young man, he developed the thinking that until one could earn three or four times of the amount enough for his survival, one should not think of inviting a girl into his life. He led life in such a harsh reality.

'But, today a girl is asking me to marry her!.... she is highly educated!... came from a decent brought up and background!...she is beautiful!....matured and normal!....she earning more than me!...but still she wants me!...why?....Is this what they say love?.... or gratitude for rescuing her in that incident?...but if it is so, she has saved my life and given me a future too...she saw that I have been pulled out of this case...because of her, I escaped from jail sentence and now leading a decent and contended life!...all these are more than enough for her to pay back me!...and still she likes me!...wants to marry me!...this is something difficult to understand', Rahul felt.

He came out of his thoughts as his mobile started ringing.

It's from Sheela!

His heart started beating high.

"Hello Sheela!", Rahul tried to keep a low voice.

"Happy New year Rahul! And also Wish you a very happy and a very Special birthday!", Sheela's voice is so sweet.

"Oh! How do you know it!?", Rahul wondered.

"That's a silly question!", Sheela intervened in an official tone.

Rahul liked the way she handles him so possessively.

"Thank you Sheela! Thanks for the wishes!...And I too wish you a very happy New year!", Rahul reciprocated in a soft and gentle voice.

"Oh! My God!...You've already started to be nice and gentle!.. Responding well and reciprocating wishes too!... That's great!", Sheela is at her usual teasing mood.

"Nothing like that Sheela! I'm normal", Rahul tried to hide blushing signs in his voice.

"That's Okay...by the way.....Get ready and be here by ten thirty sharp!....we'll be waiting for you...and come with a sweet packet and some fruits...Got it!", Sheela ordered.

"Sheela...if you don't mind...I want to ask you something", Rahul slowly asked like a kid mustering courage.

"Go ahead!", Sheela encouraged him mischievously.

"You have come from a decent family...Highly educated...beautiful....doing a good job! Earning well!....Why do you like me?...Do you think that.... I'm....a suitable match.... for you...What's my background?...I'm an orphan!...had involved in illegal activities and came out of the case thanks to your kindness!... Then how could I be suitable for you?", Rahul asked in a meek voice holding his breath.

Sheela is silent for a few seconds and responded, "Do you think that I knew nothing about you? I have been seeing you even before that bad incident!...you know?...Since your childhood, circumstances have pushed you into hardships!...Haunting loneliness has taught you tough lessons about the value of life!..... That's why, you're like this today!... And about liking you....hmm!....you know one thing!......Any girl falls for you Rahul!...you know why?...you're such a golden boy!....you tend to keep minding your own business even being thrown into a bunch of beautiful girls!....that's what girls do like....particularly girls like me!...but, you're such a dumb log who doesn't know how to deal with and approach a girl who falls for you...isn't it?.... hmm!...I'll have to work so hard to tune up you into a normal man!....that's my new year's resolution!...so, don't think too much...we're not in teenage!....we're grown up!...get ready and be here by the time...Okay...and by the way, don't smoke before coming here...Okay!", Sheela cut the call.

His mind filled with such a joyous feeling he has never experienced before. He felt so confident and ambitious about his life and its future purpose. Rahul looked at his mobile. It's already eight fifteen. He got up from the bed and went to bathroom hurriedly. It took him more than one hour to get ready. He opened the paper bag received from Sheela and took out the shirt. He tucked it in a black cotton jeans.

Rahul stood before the mirror. He saw in the mirror a handsome young man standing elegantly in a bright sky blue color branded formal shirt that is well fitted and really made him looking so good. The regular workouts and jogging made him fit and strong. He liked his face looking in the mirror with a trimmed beard and a neat hairstyle. Everything looked right in his face.

'Yes, I'm Good!, She is right!', Rahul felt satisfied looking at his image.

****

The End

www.ingramcontent.com/pod-product-compliance
Lightning Source LLC
La Vergne TN
LVHW091207150826
845672LV00005B/1278

9798891335141